The Black Stallion Legend

When tragedy strikes in the life of young Alec Ramsay, he flees blindly west, taking only his beloved black stallion with him. Deep in the southwestern desert he stumbles on an isolated tribe of Indians who have a startling legend—that at the end of the world a rider on a black horse will appear and lead them to safety.

Alec wants no part of this fearful prophecy. But then a mammoth upheaval shatters the land, and he and the Black are helplessly caught up in the tribe's fate. . . .

The Black Stallion Legend

BY WALTER FARLEY

Random House New York

Library of Congress Cataloging in Publication Data:

Farley, Walter
   The Black Stallion legend.
   SUMMARY: The Black Stallion helps save an Indian tribe during a
time of disaster, thereby fulfilling an ancient prophecy.
   [1. Horses—Fiction.   2. Indians of North America—Fiction]
I. Title   II. Series.
PZ7.F236Bk   1983   [Fic]   83-1870

ISBN: 0–394–86026–8 (trade hardcover)
        0–394–96026–2 (library binding)

Manufactured in the United States of America
1   2   3   4   5   6   7   8   9   0

For Rosemary

Contents

The Black Stallion Legend

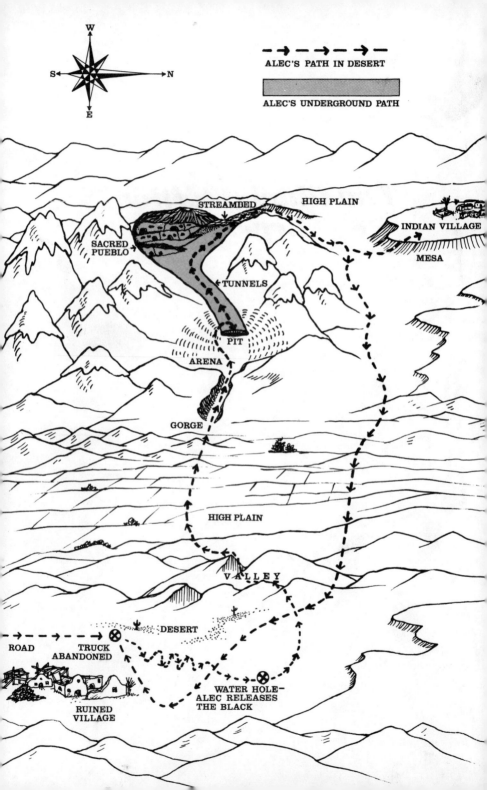

Winter Rider

1

Alec Ramsay jogged around the racecourse infield, his body very lean and taut beneath a heavy woolen sweat suit. The temperature was below freezing and the racing strip alongside him was flanked by ice and snow. A frigid wind blew down the stretch and he lowered his hooded head against it.

Alec thought of himself as an outdoorsman and stayed indoors only when necessary. He jogged all year long to keep in shape, to keep his wind. A jockey needed strong legs and good wind. Jogging opened your lungs. It helped in the afternoon, when you raced.

But that morning's conditions were not normal even for December in New York, and Alec would have much preferred clear skies and a little higher temperature. While racing held many good memories for him, it also had taken its toll, just as it had for many other jockeys he knew. His hands were strong, thick and calloused, capable of moving with the quick skill of a musician—yet he felt an excruciating pain between the first two fingers of each hand where he held the reins when he rode.

It was arthritis, the doctor had told him, which would be especially painful during the winter months. Alec shook his hooded head in dismay. Arthritis (which he had always associated with older people) while still a young man! To say nothing of the calcified pain he suffered from a mended collarbone. But falls and broken bones were part of racing. There would be still more pain in the years to come. How much physical resilience was left in his body? Alec wondered. How much longer could he go on?

Alec had a good view of the Aqueduct's empty grandstand and clubhouse as he jogged down the long stretch. High above the tiered floors and glass-encased newsroom were the videotape cameras fixed at the edge of the clubhouse roof. His gaze shifted to the track on the other side of the infield rail. It was sloppy with a light snow falling on it. He knew that today every rider should concentrate more on surviving than winning races. But that wouldn't be. They had to race to win. And soon, for it was only three hours before the first race of the afternoon, the stands would be filled with thousands of hardy fans who could have stayed at home.

Alec buried his face in the hood and lowered his eyes to the snowy ground before him. While he had to be there, he couldn't be blamed for envying the riders who were racing in Florida and California during these cold winter months. Despite his sweating, he was wearing too much clothing to get loose the way he should. His knees were beginning to bother him too, and he hoped he wasn't getting water on the knee like some of the other jocks. Anyway, he had a nice, warm whirlpool bath and a steam box to look forward to when he got to the jocks' room. He'd get loosened up that way and lose a few more pounds while at it.

Alec hoped he'd be able to get down to 104 pounds today. If he didn't, Henry Dailey would have his head as a Christmas present. Their filly, Pam's Song, was the lightweight in the race, assigned only 110 pounds, which meant with six pounds of tack Alec had to step on the scales weighing no more than 104, six pounds less than his usual weight. That was another reason for jogging and jogging and jogging.

It gave him time to think, too, before riding. One had very little time to think on a racehorse. You just *did* it, moved when you had to move. His thoughts turned to Pam's Song, the beautiful, strapping filly he would ride—a burnished blonde shade of chestnut, the color of her dam, not her sire, the Black. Yes, and the color too of the golden hair of her namesake, Pam. But he shouldn't let himself think too much about Pam today, for Henry had told him it affected his riding. Henry was right. When Alec thought of the girl he loved, it was difficult to keep his mind on anything else.

Pam had left Hopeful Farm for Europe over a month ago, leaving behind memories so vivid they would always be a part of him.* But Alec wanted more than that. He wanted to be with her during the Christmas break. This was the last day of the track meeting and he looked forward to a two-week vacation before racing resumed in January. If he could get away from duties at Hopeful Farm, he would fly to Europe if only for a few days. He had named the beautiful filly for Pam as a Christmas present to her.

Alec's gaze turned once more to the empty stands as he recalled the dark Saturday afternoon in November when Aqueduct was jam-packed with eighty thousand people watching the running of the classic Empire State Handicap. Pam had raced the Black that day— to prove to herself as well as to Henry and the huge throng of fans that she could hold her own with any male jockey in the land.

Later, back at Hopeful Farm, she had said, "Letting me ride the Black was the greatest thing you could have done for anyone."

Alec remembered his answer. "You're not just anyone, Pam. I love you."

"And I love you, Alec. More now than ever because I know what you gave up for me."

"I don't want you to go, Pam. I want you to stay. We'll get married."

He never doubted her love but it hadn't been enough

*The Black Stallion and the Girl

to keep her with him. Pam wanted more time to seek
out new experiences and challenges, all that life offered one as young as she.

"It's too soon for both of us," she had told him with
tears welling in her eyes. "I'm not ready for marriage
even if you think we are, Alec. And I think too much
of marriage not to be ready for it. It's the greatest
challenge I'll ever know and I want to make it work.
I want to have more to give you than I can give you
now. Please, Alec," she pleaded. "I want to stay here
with you but don't let me change my mind. Let me
grow up a little more, then we'll be together always."

When she'd finished, the tears were falling over her
high cheekbones and down her face. Alec had put his
arms around her and held her close, feeling emotions
that went deeper than any he had ever known.

"I understand, Pam. I'll wait a while and then come
after you."

"That will be best of all . . ."

Alec shook his hooded head and wiped the wet snow
from his face with a gloved hand. He had to stop
thinking of Pam or he might make the riding mistakes
Henry predicted. The old trainer had told him repeatedly, "It's no time to think of Pam or anything but
your work, Alec! This is a tough business. Keep your
mind on it!"

Racing was no longer a sport but a business to both
of them. It had to be with all their farm and racing
expenses. But Alec did not like to be shouted at or

treated like a boy. He was a man and he knew exactly where he was going and what he had to do. Today's race, the Merry Christmas Handicap for three-year-old fillies at a distance of six furlongs, only a few hours away, was part of it.

Alec jogged off the infield, heading for the jockeys' room and the warm whirlpool bath that awaited him.

Post Time!

2

Later that afternoon, with the horses in the paddock for the running of the Merry Christmas Handicap, the public address announcer gave the final weight changes for the race, concluding with "number eight, Pam's Song, three pounds over."

Henry Dailey tightened the cinch about the filly's girth and growled at Alec Ramsay. "You coulda made 110."

"I couldn't," Alec said. "I sweated off all I could."

"Three pounds less would have made a big difference in this race," the trainer retorted.

"I'm sorry," the jockey said. "I did the best I could." Alec didn't like to be scolded by his old friend but there wasn't much he could do about it—except to understand the reasons for Henry's tirade. It wouldn't have been different with another trainer. Weights were

9

assigned by the track handicapper in an attempt to bring all the horses in a race down to the finish line together. They were an important part of the game and despite a jockey's ability to ride, a trainer looked elsewhere when a rider could not make the assigned weight for his horse.

Once upon a time, Alec had thought that success was having the money to buy what he wanted, including horses, and the freedom to enjoy them. But it wasn't. He had learned that to be successful in business called for a lot of self-denial, whether one was talking about personal comfort or self-interest. He had to do what was expected of him.

Henry straightened after making certain the saddle was secure, and turned to Alec. He studied the face of the young man in the black-and-white-checkered racing silks. "You know what to do," he said. It was not a question and only required Alec's confirmation of what was expected of him in the race.

"I know," Alec said quietly. "I'm just afraid she won't like the track today. Despite the cold it's soft in spots and she'll slide."

"Don't worry about it," Henry said. "She'll do okay. She's going to be Aqueduct's horse of the winter."

"If you say so."

Henry didn't like the way Alec said it, or the way he looked. Alec's face was thin, good-looking, unlined and set off by prominent, even teeth that flashed whenever he smiled, which wasn't too often these days. The same thing went for his eyes, blue and usually laughing; but lately the skin was stretched drum-tight across his cheekbones, making his eyes seem sunken and piercing. He looked tired, despite his healthy body.

The old trainer smiled suddenly and put his arm around the young man's shoulders. "I didn't mean to get sore about your weight," he said kindly. "Maybe we lost some advantage over the rest of the field, but we can still whip 'em."

Alec knew Henry wasn't apologizing but appeasing him, comforting him so he would ride this race as he should and bring the filly home a winner. Winning a big stake race was important to Henry and, of course, to Hopeful Farm. The better their horses raced, the more money their yearlings would bring at the sales, where prices were already setting records.

For Alec, what mattered was not the size or importance of a race or the price yearlings got at auction, but bringing home a winner. His biggest thrill was winning races where he never thought he had a chance. And, contrary to Henry's expectations of the filly, Alec thought this race might be tough to win. He might not succeed but he'd been beaten before in big races.

Alec raised a leg and Henry boosted him into the saddle. He stroked the filly's neck, quieting her.

Pam's Song was tall, already over sixteen hands, and still a little ungainly for her size. She jumped and played a little, enjoying the snow, as Henry led her about the walking ring with the other horses in the field of eight going to the post.

They'd soon find out if Pam's Song liked to run in

bad weather, Alec decided. Today's race was something of a proving ground for her. A little over three months ago she had been a nonentity in the Hopeful Farm Stable, a good-looking sort of big, lazy filly, one of many at the farm, promising but not proven. Then they had raced her conservatively in three races where the competition had not been tough, and she had won all of them. This was to be her first major race on a cold and very windy day, which Henry thought to her liking.

Alec kept stroking the filly's neck, telling her to settle down, that the time for play was over. She'd acted the same way on the track that morning when he had loosened her up. It was a good sign to Alec, for a horse had to enjoy life, the same as a person. If a horse wasn't happy, he wouldn't run for you. So maybe Henry was right. Maybe Pam's Song would be Aqueduct's horse of the winter. At any rate, Henry wasn't going to send her south for the winter or, for that matter, even out of New York City.

Alec looked at the seven other horses in the paddock walking ring. Six of them were the very best of those who had stayed north during the winter, and the remaining one had come up from Florida just for this race. Her name was Delta Belle and she was the favorite, carrying the heaviest weight in the field at 118 pounds. She had been one of the top two-year-olds racing last year and had won her first three races at Gulfstream Park in Florida. Delta Belle was being ridden by her regular jockey, Eduardo Gomez, who didn't look too happy with the day's weather after having spent several months in the sunny southland.

Henry said, "You got two choices, Alec. If she breaks sharp, go on with her. If she doesn't, just let her settle down and get her clear."

Alec met Henry's gaze, eyes that still held the fire and gusto of youth despite the mass of wrinkles that crisscrossed the old man's face. Henry looked like what he was, one of the nicest and best-liked trainers ever to saddle a horse. To others he appeared calm, patient and kind. But Alec knew otherwise. Henry was hypersensitive, a bundle of nervous energy and a perfectionist. Nothing was ever done quite the way *he* wanted, the way only *he* could do it. And Henry did everything but ride. That morning he had gone non-stop despite the cold, applying bandages, walking the filly back from the track, even taking her away from Alec to cool her out.

There was no changing Henry, Alec knew, but the old professional, who was his closest friend, could make mistakes the same as the rest of them.

Henry left them at the track and Alec rode Pam's Song in her eighth position to the post. He knew he had a real nice horse under him and Henry had done a good job training her—but he didn't have Henry's complete confidence that she was ready for the kind of competition she faced today. He hoped he was wrong. It would be easier to get along with Henry if Pam's Song kept the old man's adrenaline flowing during the winter months.

The filly shifted quickly beneath him and he had trouble keeping his seat as she slid in the snow. She was too eager, as always. Just as she was used to doing things her own way; that was why Alec found it hard to rate her speed during a race. She had a mind of her own. Alec knew that was why he had named her Pam's Song, for she was a lot like his beloved Pam.

Don't think of Pam now, he reminded himself, *not now.*

Alec had been successful recently in getting the filly to race the way he wanted—sometimes anyway. He didn't know what she'd be like today. With her blazing speed, there was no doubt she'd be first out of the gate and she'd fight him if he tried to take her back.

His fingers were cold and stiff and painful as he knotted the reins. He wiped off his goggles and adjusted them more securely about his helmet. The snow had stopped falling but the gale-force wind almost swept him out of the saddle. He ignored the wind as he did the pain in his fingers, knowing it was no different for the other riders. He kept his mind on his horse and the race to be run.

Behind the starting gate, an assistant starter took hold of Pam's Song's bridle and, lifting his rubber-booted legs heavily out of the slop, led her into the number 8 starting stall.

The Merry Christmas Handicap

3

Pam's Song banged against the sides of her starting stall and Alec spoke to her softly, telling her to be patient. They were in the far outside stall; it was better, Alec knew, than being close to the rail where he might be pinned against it. With this kind of track he needed all the room he could get.

The race was being started from the six-furlong pole on the far side of the track. Across the snow-piled infield Alec could see the stands, now jammed with thousands of fans despite a day that was close to being a snow disaster. While few cars were getting through on the Long Island expressways, trains had brought the crowd to Aqueduct. It was these fans who made New York the most important center of racing in America. How New York fared not only affected racing as a whole but also influenced breeding and the sale prices of yearlings, of broodmares, of stallion shares and breeding. That's why Henry was interested in staying there and racing. It was the place to be, bad weather or not.

Alec steadied Pam's Song. Within a few seconds he'd have a lot of decisions to make, and he'd have to make them quickly in a race as short as six furlongs. If he hesitated, he'd lose the race. He had to avoid jams. He had to sense what was going to happen *before* it happened.

"Easy, girl, easy," he said softly as Pam's Song twisted in her stall, upsetting his balance as well as her own. "Easy."

Henry thought Pam's Song was easy to race but Alec knew different. No one knows a horse better than the person sitting on his back. No horse stayed the same from day to day any more than people did. You had to ride them as you found them that day. A horse might stop running for you one day and go the distance the next. Pam's Song had class and ability, but she needed good hands and patience, and if everything didn't go just right for her, she might not do her best.

"Run for me today, baby," he whispered in the filly's ear. "Run for me."

Suddenly Delta Belle in the next stall broke through the grilled door, delaying the start. She ran only a short distance before a red-coated outrider caught her bridle and brought her back. Alec studied her every movement; judging other horses was as important as knowing his own.

Delta Belle was a walloper in size—a rich, dark bay, almost black in color. She looked more like a colt than a filly, a truly big horse with wonderful leverage of the hind legs, even at the slow trot with which she came back to the starting gate. To Alec this meant enormous propulsion when she did run. The rest of her body, too, gave the impression of power. She was not a showy horse but very plain with a large Roman nose, curved and protruding. Her shoulders were well laid back and her limbs, unlike those of his own mount who was still developing, were in proper proportion to her great size. This horse, the favorite in the race, would give trouble to any three-year-old in the country, including the colts.

Alec stroked his filly's neck. She had lost her skittishness and was quiet, maybe too quiet. "Wake up, girl," he said. "Don't go to sleep on me now."

Delta Belle was being led into her stall and Alec studied her rider, Eduardo Gomez, whom he knew only by reputation. Gomez was no different from most of the other young riders who had come up from racing in countries south of the United States. Gomez was Panamanian, just eighteen and very hungry to win races. He rode Delta Belle into her starting stall, his long black hair hanging from beneath his protective helmet.

Gomez caught Alec watching him and grinned. "She not happy with this weather," he said. "Me too. We win. We go."

Alec smiled back but said nothing. He studied

Gomez's face for some indication of what the other jockey planned to do. But there was nothing to see in the Panamanian's face, just dark skin, high cheekbones, sunken eyes, making him look ravaged and hungry despite his incredible success this year riding. No doubt that the lean, poverty-stricken years behind him had left their mark and would always remain a part of him.

There was a loud thump, then lots of yelling, as another horse broke through the gate. But once again an alert outrider was there to head the horse off and bring her back.

Pam's Song banged impatiently against the sides of her stall, and Alec said, "Too bad, but we have to wait a little longer. Easy, girl." He hoped she was listening to him.

It was the number 4 horse coming back, Iron Flight, an iron-gray filly, her coat gleaming with obvious good health. She'd come up from the Maryland tracks, where she'd won her last five starts and was the second favorite in the race. She was small but solidly built, and had gotten into the race with 114 pounds, four less than Delta Belle. Alec knew she'd be a hard one to beat.

It made no difference to Alec, as it did to Henry, that a girl rode Iron Flight. Henry had little use for women at the racetrack, even as grooms. That was why he'd been glad to see Pam go.

Don't think of Pam now, Alec cautioned himself again.

But his eyes followed the girl in Iron Flight's saddle,

knowing Liz Smith could ride with the best of the men. He had seen her race a few times in New York but she rode mostly at the Maryland and Delaware tracks, where she got more mounts. She'd waited a long time for this particular horse, for as she'd told Alec earlier, "I've hoped all along to get a two-year-old with class and ride him all the way through his career." She was doing it with this filly, having lost only one race on Iron Flight last year at two, and going undefeated this year at three. But this was the first time she was meeting a horse of Delta Belle's quality.

Or my filly, Alec reminded himself. He stroked Pam's Song's neck. His mount was being good, very good; only another minute or so now and they'd be off.

Alec watched Liz Smith as she rode past him to go back into the gate. He saw the wisp of blonde hair hanging from beneath her red-checkered helmet with the green pompon, then the flashing blue eyes as she removed her goggles to readjust them. She was small-boned, fragile-looking, but Alec was aware of her strength, as he had been of Pam's. Everything about this girl's appearance reminded him of Pam and he felt his great loneliness and the emptiness that went with it. But he'd be with Pam soon, he reminded himself, very soon.

Pam had surmounted the same obstacles as had Liz—sexism on the racetrack. Men such as Henry, who wouldn't put a girl on a horse's back, not in the afternoon anyway. Male jockeys who didn't regard women as a threat, even when they did get a mount to race.

But Alec was not one of them. Pam had taught him many things, and some had to do with racing. It took balance and instinct and intelligence, as well as strength, to ride 1,200 pounds of horse going at top speed. And women riders were as well equipped as men to guide them. It also took great ability to make a horse relax, to have him want to do his best for you. And in this respect, women were often better equipped than men. At least, it had been so with Pam, Alec knew. Horses ran for her.

But stop thinking of Pam. It's no time—

The gate door flew open, the bell clanged. The Merry Christmas Handicap was on and Alec knew he'd been caught unprepared for the start! From behind the chestnut filly's braided mane, he saw the other horses break in front of him, the slop and shouts of their riders flying through the air.

Delta Belle had broken well from her number 7 stall and Gomez was outracing Iron Flight into the lead. But Liz Smith wasn't letting her small, iron-gray filly fall behind and was moving Iron Flight as fast as she could go. Apparently she was going to make a speed duel of it early.

Alec knew it had been his fault that Pam's Song hadn't broken as sharply from the gate as she should. Henry would be aware of it and would probably know the reason for it. But all that would come later.

Alec moved Pam's Song to the middle of the track, now that she'd found her stride. But she wasn't grabbing the track as she should, and Alec knew it wasn't to her liking.

"Easy, baby, easy," he called, trying to relax her. "Plenty of time yet." The distance down the backstretch to the far turn was one quarter of a mile, around the turn itself was another quarter mile, and then a final quarter down the homestretch to the finish line.

Through his filly's pitched ears Alec saw Delta Belle begin to draw clear of Iron Flight and the rest of the field. Delta Belle was running easily, smoothly, confidently, as if Gomez knew the race was already his, having fought off Iron Flight's challenge successfully. Liz Smith had dropped her iron-gray filly back to fourth place and it looked like she was finished. Alec moved Pam's Song up alongside her, knowing he was in a good position and planning to stay in the clear until later when he would move on again. He wanted to save his filly's final effort for the homestretch. She was running easily and responding to his hands. She'd have plenty left for the finish.

The field of seven horses running behind Delta Belle bunched closer approaching the turn, with snow and water splashing on every side of them. A hard-running roan filly pulled up on Alec's right side, challenging the leaders, her rider whooping and hollering. His shouts stirred up Pam's Song and Alec felt his filly grab for the bit.

"Shut up!" he yelled at the other jockey, knowing it would do no good but saying it anyway. He took hold of Pam's Song, pulling her up, not wanting to go any faster. It was then that he felt the saddle slip beneath him, going forward until it was halfway off the saddlecloth! Alec reached back, clawing at the saddle-cloth, but it was to no avail. With the saddle riding high on the filly's withers, he had no control over his mount!

Pam's Song moved forward with an unleashed burst of speed, moving ahead of Iron Flight and the others in blinding pursuit of Delta Belle only three lengths ahead.

She caught the favorite before they'd reached the turn, and with still a half-mile to go! Alec knew it was too far to go all out, as she was doing, and win. He had no choice but to stay on her, if he could, let alone pull her up. Never before had a saddle slipped on him during a race. Henry had not secured it properly or the water splashing against her belly had stretched the elastic. Either way, nothing could be done now except to hang on!

Delta Belle increased her speed as Pam's Song pulled alongside, her jockey glancing at the chestnut filly's bobbing head beside him, then urging his favorite on.

They swept around the turn, going stride for stride as a two-horse team. Alec couldn't understand the reason for Gomez wanting this speed vendetta with him, unless the other jockey hadn't noticed that he had no control over Pam's Song. Whatever the reason, it was obvious that Delta Belle had not met this kind of challenge deep in the stretch in a major race and was digging in, fighting back, refusing to give up the lead. Pam's Song was inching ahead of the favorite but Alec knew she couldn't maintain this torrid pace much longer—and neither could Delta Belle.

Passing the stands with less than a furlong to go, only two hundred yards more, Alec knew what was going to happen. He heard the rush of hoofs from behind and wondered which horse it was going to be.

A low-leveled, iron-gray head drew alongside. Red-checkered silks, topped with a green pompon on a protective helmet, came in sight. Alec knew it was Iron Flight and Liz Smith who would win this race.

Pam's Song missed a stride and Alec steadied her, knowing he wasn't going to be in on the final drive to the finish wire. But neither was Delta Belle, for the blistering pace had beaten her too. The favorite was faltering, giving way, despite the whipping she was getting from Gomez.

"Go get it, Liz!" Alec yelled as Iron Flight pulled away from both of them.

Alec didn't urge Pam's Song on, while Delta Belle responded to Gomez's whip by coming on again to finish second to the iron-gray filly. It was enough, Alec decided, that they were third, and that they had been able to finish the race at all.

Ahead of him was a vacation, and time to be with Pam. He desperately needed both.

The Loss

4

Deep snow covered the paddocks and pastures of Hopeful Farm but horses were turned out and playing beneath a bright noonday sun. Alec stood at the window of his office in the Stallion Barn and watched them. It was quiet, very quiet, and the contrast to the daily noise at the racetrack acted as a tranquilizer. The peace of it was made all the more beautiful because he had left Henry behind at Aqueduct.

His old friend had been furious with him for being caught napping at the start of the race, telling him the saddle wouldn't have slipped had he been clear from the start and not bunched with the others where the going had been sloppiest of all. Henry never took into account that he might not have secured the saddle as well as he should have done.

"Finish up what you have to do at the farm," he

had bellowed. "Then go see *that girl* and get her out of your system. That's if you want to ride for me!" It was just like the old man to blame anyone but himself for what went wrong these days. Henry had been under a lot of pressure lately, financial pressure most of all.

Hopeful Farm was an incorporated business with Alec's parents and Henry as principal stockholders. Officially, Alec's position was that of stable rider, since one could not own and ride a racehorse. Unofficially, Alec was as much under pressure as anyone else, for races had to be won if the farm was going to remain in business.

Alec pictured Henry after the race, all stooped over with his arms hanging down like an ape's, saying, "You could have pushed her on and taken second money from Delta Belle; that would have meant eleven thousand dollars instead of only six thousand." Henry had been more hard-eyed than ever, and there had been a sickly pallor to his face. The pressure was telling on both of them, Alec knew. It wasn't what Hopeful Farm was meant to be for them, not at all.

He watched the mares in the adjacent field, all heavy in foal to the Black or Satan. The future of Hopeful Farm rested on the colts and fillies they were carrying. Would he and Henry be able to hold out, to wait for these foals to win races or bring sales prices that would keep them going? Only time would tell.

Meanwhile, Alec regretted that their great need for dollars had turned his love for horses into a business. It had changed him, just as it had Henry.

Who could say what he truly wanted anymore? Except something he didn't have yet. Something just over the hill. Something just beyond the reach of his fingertips. He didn't know what he was after. He was worse than Henry, who *did* know. A few years ago all Alec truly wanted was to race. Then he'd got the chance, just as Henry had, thanks to the Black. But there should be more between them than what there was. They were still friends but not the way they used to be, and their need for money was the reason for it.

Henry didn't mean it when he'd said he'd get other riders. Not that he couldn't, Alec knew. Every jock on the grounds was panting for a chance to ride for Henry, who could do as much for a jockey as he could a horse. He'd told Alec, "You're gaining experience and maturing as a rider, but you still have a way to go. The great thing is that you're as good as you are so soon." And then, when he'd seen Alec's face fall, he'd fretted and massaged his cheeks with one hand before adding, "Not that I can find fault with you when you ride the Black. That's different. You're tattooed on him; *you're one with him*. It's the other horses I'm talking about."

Alec turned away from the window and went back to his desk. He didn't want to think about it anymore. He was tired, exhausted, as whipped mentally and emotionally as Henry. It was good to be alone, to be able to just put his head down on the desk and close his eyes, to do nothing but think of the girl he loved and what might have been . . . or what still might be.

There was no sound in the room except Alec's deep breathing as he tried to relax every race-torn muscle. He had no trouble controlling his body. It was his head that was giving him problems. He *needed* Pam.

Alec saw her again. Every feature, every detail, was there in his mind. But it was not her golden hair, her long-lashed blue eyes, her high, sharp cheekbones or her ears as small and delicately sculptured as her nose that meant most to him. No, it was none of these that he remembered so well, that made him want to walk beside her forever. It was her will to live and the joy she brought to him and all those she touched. It was her honesty, every emotion showing clearly in her face, with nothing to hide or to prove to anyone, seeing only one person, one thought at a time, talking, describing her life, speaking with all the spontaneity and excitement of a child, *"I live! I live!"*

A face so different from his own, Alec thought, and from all those he knew. In his everyday, workaday world he wore a mask, and even when startled, surprised, frightened, nothing showed. The mask hid his inner self and he worked efficiently, emotionlessly, from day to day.

Alec raised his head from the desk. He needed to be touched by Pam's magic again, to feel her sense of sureness, of rightness, her softness yet resilience, her gaiety yet earnestness. All this he needed to survive the pressures he felt engulfing him.

Alec opened a desk drawer and removed a stack of letters he had received from Pam. Taking the last one, he opened the envelope and read:

> 18, *Quai de Béthune*
> *Paris, France*
> *Dec. 12th*

Dear Alec,
    *I can't wait to see you! It's been so long! I love you
and want to be with you always . . .*

Alec stopped reading and wondered, did that mean she was ready to come back? She'd been working at stables in England and France for almost two months. Maybe she'd had enough. Maybe she'd return with him to Hopeful Farm!

> *. . . I've been so happy lately I can hardly stay in
my skin. I've been grooming horses in the neatest riding school just outside Paris, where they teach dres-
sage. Part of my salary has gone into riding lessons
naturally. Oh, Alec, I know what joy it is for you to
ride a fast racehorse, but did you know you can achieve
the same joy from riding at a slow, cadenced trot? It's
called "passage," and you're truly one with your horse.
It's the same feeling as when you ride the Black, only
you achieve it by high, measured strides. I can't wait
to have you try it! We have Hanoverians, Trakehners,
even Lipizzaners to ride when you get here! . . .*

Alec paused again. He'd never heard of Hanoverians or Trakehners but knew of the Lipizzaners at the Spanish Riding School in Vienna, Austria. Pam's love for horses included all breeds and all kinds of riding, Western as well as English. There was no one horse for her, as the Black was for him. She was a natural horsewoman, gifted with an instinctive understanding of the equine mind.

Pam loved all people as she did all breeds of horses, Alec reminded himself. She wanted to try everything, know everybody, not waste a minute of her time, her life. She wanted to enjoy each moment, each day, each horse and each face. How could she settle for one person, one kind of life with him? Alec wondered. He knew she loved him as he did her, but would it ever work out? It would, he decided, if he thought of marriage as not being mutual ownership. If he always respected Pam as the complete individual that she was and understood her love and need to expand. He had no doubt that he could do it. Pam's response to life, her exuberance, her trust in her fellow man, was what made him love her all the more.

    . . . *Three friends and I have rented a small Volkswagen and are leaving tomorrow for the Spanish Riding School in Vienna to see the Lipizzaners perform! We'll be gone only a week, and I'll be back by the time you get here. We're going by way of the highest Alps through Austria, and the beauty of the snow-covered mountains and passes should be something to see! It's snowing here in Paris so it should be really great up there! I wish you were going with me, but we'll have our time together, Alec, and it will be forever. Ours is not a story with a beginning and an ending. Didn't I always love you? Won't I always?*

                                                    Pam

Alec put the letters away. The difficult part of being in love, he thought, was letting go when and if necessary. One can never *have* or *own* anyone. But he needed Pam very much, now more than ever. How he wanted to forget the necessity for winning, the frustration of losing. How he hated the fact that, from a business point of view, so much money was invested in him to win. He knew that if he didn't get away he'd break under the mental strain and be no good to Hopeful Farm or anyone else. Only Pam could help him break free of the pressures that had him imprisoned. He needed to feel her joy again, the joy of life itself and all it offered.

Alec left the office and went to his horses. Walking past the stalls, he smelled again all the familiar odors he loved—of hay, ammonia and feed—and heard the familiar sounds. Satan nickered and came to the iron bars of his stall, eager for attention. Even after so short a time away from the farm, Alec was impressed by Satan's size. He had put on more weight and was huge compared to the Black, so massive, so powerful in chest and shoulders. His head was large, too, larger than his sire's, but fine in nose and muzzle.

Alec spoke softly to him, reaching through the bars

to rub the white, diamond-shaped star in the center of his forehead. He remained with the big horse only a few more minutes before moving down the corridor.

Alec loved Satan but not the way he loved his sire, the Black. Satan was Henry's horse. As far as the trainer was concerned, Satan was the best horse they'd ever owned. Henry had molded him into a superb racing machine, one that was very competitive yet willing to obey the slightest touch of rein or leg. And for that reason, too, Satan had become a superb stud horse. He was too well trained to act the fighter when he passed another stallion or some innocent mare in a stall. He knew what was his and what wasn't. And most important of all, he was content with his life at the farm, making him easy to handle.

It was far different with the Black. He was always on his toes, conscious of every step, every whisper in the barn, and ready to challenge anyone who came near him. Neither Alec nor anyone else had ever *made* anything of the Black. He was more tamed than trained. And tamed only because Alec asked and the stallion gave. One did not fight the Black.

Alec stopped before the stallion's stall. The Black stood before the open window with the rays of the sun streaming upon his body. Alec spoke to him, his voice low and gentle. A muscle quivered in the horse's marvelously smooth skin, then another and still another. But he did not turn away from the window.

Alec knew his horse was aware of him and he spoke to him again. The Black's chest swelled, his nostrils trembled; then he turned toward Alec, his eyes lighting up as he moved across the stall.

Going inside, Alec pulled down the Black's head to his own and stroked him, his fingers finding spots he knew gave his horse much pleasure and contentment because he could not reach them himself. The Black lowered his head still more so Alec might rub beneath his small ears. Alec held him close. It was good to be with his horse, where he belonged.

The Black bent his long, graceful neck, his nostrils quivering and sniffing. He remained still, enjoying Alec's touches while his long tail switched contentedly. Never was there a more magnificent horse, Alec knew. The Black was a perfect specimen, perfectly balanced, perfectly muscled. And he was as intelligent as he was well made. Too smart to bow to the will of Henry or anyone else. Too much a lover of freedom to be confined to a stall. The Black thrived best on blowing wind and green grass.

"I'm sorry," Alec said quietly. "I didn't mean it to turn out this way, but there's no turning back for us. We're in it too deep. I don't know what it would take for us to be *free* again—like it was, once upon a time."

Alec studied the Black. The horse might not be enjoying his confinement but he'd kept in shape by exercising himself in the large paddocks. There was no fat on him. Nor did he look drawn, creased or worn out from all the racing he'd done. There was a sharpness and spring to his every movement that matched the alertness in his eyes. Alec knew the Black was in good racing condition despite his being away from the track.

The stallion cocked his ears as Alec continued talking to him, the words making little sense most of the time with only the sounds and rhythm being important. In this way they communicated with each other. The Black whinnied in reply, his long nostrils distended, his eyes bold.

"I wish you were going to France with me, but I'll be away only a few days. I can't take you this time. When I get back, we'll do something together that's fun, really fun, I promise you."

But, Alec wondered, *should I promise? Can I have fun with him when I get back? What about Henry? What about all that's ahead?* He had responsibilities. And with the breeding season coming up in February, the Black had responsibilities as well. Yet, Alec thought, there would be a slowing down of work between Christmas and February. If he could just get out of racing so much, perhaps he and the Black could get away together if only for a short time.

Suddenly the Black raised his head from Alec's arms, his small ears cocked and listening. Then he whinnied to the mares he'd heard outside. He went to the window and looked out, a coal-black silhouette against the golden light of the sun. Becoming more excited, he uttered a shrill whistle that was clearly meant for the mares he could not see but knew were there. He gathered himself, rocked back on his hindquarters and plunged about the stall, almost knocking Alec over.

Alec left the stall, knowing he could do nothing to distract the Black from the mares outside. "You be good," he said. "I'll be back soon and then we'll go away. Somehow we'll go away somewhere, if only for a few days."

Outside the barn he plodded through the deep snow of the driveway. He wanted to pick up the mail to find out if there was a last letter from Pam before he drove to Kennedy Airport in New York City. Back in the office was his plane ticket, and his bag was packed and ready. Now that he'd been with the Black he'd said his good-byes to everybody. No one would miss him for a while.

Alec looked at the broodmares on the other side of the driveway fence. They were listening to the Black's calls from the Stallion Barn. So it is with life, Alec thought, and with one's *need* for another. One needed one for balance.

"Oh, Pam, soon we'll be together," he said aloud.

Reaching into the mail container, he removed several letters and *The New York Times*. There was no letter from Pam, only bills addressed to the farm.

Alec walked up the driveway while opening up the newspaper to read the day's weather forecast. Snow was predicted in the afternoon, but if he left soon, he should have no trouble getting to the airport on time.

His eyes fell to a short story in the lower right-hand corner of the front page. He was attracted to it because of the *Paris, France,* dateline. Then he read:

FOUR STUDENTS KILLED IN ALPS CAR CRASH

ONE FROM U.S.

PARIS, France, December 15—Four students of the famous Phillipe de Pluminel School of Horsemanship were killed in a car crash twenty miles outside the mountain town of Kufstein, Austria. The students, Pam Athena, Denise Hermes, Simone Hachette, and Claudette Bradley, were riding in a Volkswagen when it skidded on the highest road in the Alps and plunged into an abyss. All students were from France except Pam Athena, an American, from Venice, Florida. The students were on their way to watch the Lipizzaner horses perform at the Spanish Riding School in Vienna.

The newspaper dropped from Alec's hands. For a moment he stood quietly in the snow, feeling nothing, seeing nothing. Then from somewhere deep within him came a piercing scream, wailing and shattering the stillness of the winter day. It was never-ending as he plunged forward, head downward, seeking the board fence for support. And when he came hard against it, his wailing stopped momentarily as he screamed the words, *"You can't die! I won't let you! Pam!"*

Only the broodmares heard him. Startled, they turned their fine heads in Alec's direction. Then their short, incessant neighs echoed the sorrowful wailing that went on and on and on.

The Mourning

5

Alec remained hard against the fence, frozen like a statue. He continued screaming Pam's name but the cries from his throat were nothing but a funnel of white in the cold, cold air. He stood there in the silence, his body shaking, his ears pounding, his head throbbing. He screamed Pam's name again and this time the sound of his voice emerged from his throat, croaked and horrible.

"She . . . never . . . should have . . . gone away. I . . . I loved her . . . so much . . . so very much."

There were tears and dreadful pain in his eyes. No one could do anything to help him . . . to bring her back. His tongue and lips were beyond control and a spasm twitched the muscles of his face. He let go his deathlike grip on the fence and turned toward the barn. He could see nothing. He swayed, unable to keep his feet, and collapsed in the snow, his face blood-lessly white, his eyes as lifeless as death.

He lay in the snow in a frightening state of disin-tegration. His distress over the loss of Pam was fearful, but he knew something was wrong with his mind, something that had been triggered by his tragic loss. He could feel it. Rather, he could feel nothing, nothing at all, only the cold. Perspiration flowed from his body, dampening his skin, making him colder still. His teeth chattered as he raised his head from the snow and looked out blankly, seeing nothing.

Struggling to his feet, he held on to the top of the fence. A frigid blast of wind struck his face and he could barely open his eyes. He looked over the fence and could make out only the vague figures of the broodmares. Slowly, he maneuvered his way along the fence, holding on to it with clutched hands lest he fall again.

He went toward the Stallion Barn step by step in a dreamlike nightmare, his eyes closed. If only it *were* a dream, he thought. If only it would end when he opened his eyes. Pam would be in France waiting for him. He would go to her. They would be together again. They would be warm and safe and loving. *If only!*

He stumbled frantically through the snow. He could see almost nothing, nothing except the dim outline of the Stallion Barn, where he believed he would be safe from whatever was happening to him. Then everything went blank as he tried to move faster, weeping in his despair. He fell in the snow several more times, but always got up, struggling to his feet. He reached the barn door and threw it open.

He didn't hear the Black's neigh of welcome as he stood in the doorway, his body limp, his arms hanging straight down as if they were no longer a part of his body. He stood dazed, his eyes stark with shock.

"God," he pleaded, "please help." But no sound came from his lips.

He shook his head, trying to clear his mind, to *think*, to *see*. Even within the warm barn, he was unbearably cold, his teeth chattering. Straining his eyes, he stared at one stall after another, trying to find his horse. The intensity of his grief was something he found himself unable to cope with alone.

His voice was choked and hoarse when he found the Black's stall and called to him. But the sound of his voice was unfamiliar to the stallion who waited at the door.

Alec stood in a daze after he entered the stall. The great black horse moved toward him, and Alec threw his arms around the slender neck and held on as if never to let him go. But his cries were for Pam, and the horse's hoofs moved uneasily in the straw bedding.

The Black shoved his head hard against Alec, pushing him through the open doorway. Alec's hand slid to the halter, grasping it tightly in his great need to stay close to his horse. And he made no protests as the Black pulled him along faster once they were in the corridor, going he knew not where. Nor did he care.

Several hours later Alec's mind cleared somewhat and he found himself at the wheel of the pickup truck he used at the farm. He didn't know how he'd gotten there or where he was going. His hands trembled on the wheel as he studied the winter road before him. There was an uncertainty about his movements and the truck skidded in the snow. It was as if he couldn't remember how to do things, even drive.

What was he doing there? What had happened to him?

Half his mind was still with Pam and his thoughts paralyzed him. Alec shook his head, trying to see the road as distinctly as he saw Pam in his mind. She was standing before him, her head held high, smiling and so happy.

His eyes were full of tears as he continued looking at her. She remained as he saw her, a girl who talked with her blue eyes, her tilted head. He looked at her without touching, his eyes dwelling on her face. His body shook. She was so warm and near, so very real to him that he could feel the taste of her upon his lips. He sought to hold her, and his foot pressed down on the accelerator.

The truck slid off the road, its wheels spinning in the deep snow at the side where the snowplows had piled it. Alec banged his knee against the dashboard.

The pain was excruciating. He rammed his foot hard on the accelerator and brought the truck back to the road, the wheels spinning wildly as they hit the slick pavement. He slowed down, knowing that while he would forever see Pam in his mind, he could not touch her, *ever touch her again.*

The throbbing pain in his knee helped him see the road more clearly. It was empty of traffic. If he went slowly enough, he would not slide off it again, and he could keep going. But to where? Where was he going? What had happened to him? Shattered by shock, he knew only immense desolation.

For the first time he looked into the rearview mirror and saw his face as white as snow, his eyes stark and bloodshot. He saw also the two-horse trailer he pulled behind. His foot clamped down on the brake and he brought the truck to a stop.

What had he done in those hours between the time he had stood beside the Black in the barn and now? Had he taken his horse with him?

Leaving the truck, he went to the trailer and opened the escape door. Inside he found bags of feed and hay, and standing tied was the Black, who neighed warmly to him. Alec threw his arms around his horse and wept.

How he had loaded the Black was of no importance to him. It was enough that he had taken the Black with him. Instinctively, whatever his state of mind, he had made the Black secure in the trailer. The middle partition had been removed, allowing the stallion to spread his legs and keep his balance. Six inches of wood shavings were beneath the straw bedding to protect his feet. His legs were free of wraps, so they would not swell and heat up to cause aggravation and stomping. He had hay in his sling but no water; that would come a few hours later. And he was tied with a rubber strap so he could move about and not feel so confined.

All these things Alec had done without being aware of his movements. The truck he had taken, one of many at the farm, was powerful enough for him to have pulled the horse and trailer for several hours without being aware of it.

Alec clasped his head in his hands. His fingers kneaded the sides, hoping to clear his mind and get rid of his numbness.

Time to him now was static, like a jumped track with everything wiped clean but his love for Pam. He shut his eyes. What did it mean to have the past but not the present? He forced his eyes open. He had to go on, wherever the road led.

Leaving the trailer, he stumbled through the snow to check the hitch on the truck, making sure it was secure. Wherever he was going, nothing must happen to his horse.

He climbed behind the wheel, started the engine and drove slower and more carefully, trying to keep his anguished mind on the road.

During the hours that followed and into the night, Alec drove constantly, stopping only to get gas and to water his horse every five or six hours. His route took him south on the New York State Thruway, which was clear of snow but hazardous, and then onto the New Jersey Turnpike, where night fell upon him.

When dawn broke, he was in North Carolina on Interstate 95. He didn't know why he was headed south except, perhaps, to be free of the snow as he wanted to be free of everything else. For a moment his mind wandered to Florida and he wondered if it was to Pam's home state he wanted to go, to see her family and, perhaps, be at her funeral. He shook his head. He did not want to see one so alive, so dead. Better to see her always as she was, ever before him, smiling, beckoning him to follow her. *Where, Pam, where?*

He did not question her guidance when, hours later, he turned westward on a highway that would take him through the Deep South and ever westward.

Back at Hopeful Farm, two men stood in the Black's empty stall, their faces stricken with grief.

"He took the Black with him, Henry, that's some comfort," Alec's father said. He was much taller and several years younger than the trainer. Henry was leaning heavily against the wall of the stall as if too confused to trust his bowed legs to hold him.

"When did you first learn he hadn't gone to Paris?" Henry asked.

"Yesterday, when Hank came to my office and asked if the Black was with you at Aqueduct. I've been trying to get hold of you since then." He paused to regain his train of thought. "I went to Alec's office and found his packed bag and plane ticket. I knew something was wrong, but it wasn't until I found the newspaper in the snow and saw his tracks . . ." His gaze turned away from the trainer. "He must have fallen often in the snow, Henry," he went on finally. "The imprint of his body was all the way to the Stallion Barn."

"He read of Pam's death in the paper," the trainer said sadly. "I know how he must have felt."

"Do you?" Mr. Ramsay asked, not unkindly. "Do any of us really know?"

"He *needed* to see her," the old trainer explained. "I could tell that by his riding. He was under a lot of strain."

"We've all been under a lot of strain, too much strain."

"I pushed him too hard," Henry said regretfully. "I should have known better." Placing his hand on the taller man's arm, he added, "But I was afraid he was going to get hurt, Bill. I was worried for him. Maybe he thought different, but I knew he could be killed out there if he made many more mistakes. It's hell . . ."

"It wasn't the way Alec wanted it," the taller man said, "but that's all behind us now. I've already decided we need help to find him, Henry, *professional* help."

"The state police, you mean. Have you notified them? He can't just disappear, not driving a truck and trailer, not with a horse like the Black."

"I've been advised to be careful, very careful about what we do."

"Advised? By who?" Henry asked. "What we should

do is call the state police right now! He's been gone two days already."

"I had Dr. Warson over to the house last night, and we talked about what we should do to find Alec."

"Your friend, the psychiatrist? That's crazy!" Henry said, concerned and angry. "What good is he?"

"He's a close friend of the family," Mr. Ramsay said patiently. "He's known Alec a long time, ever since he was a little boy. It's important, David said, that we understand what's happened to Alec so we don't make things worse than they are, even lose him."

"Lose him?" Henry bellowed, unable to keep his voice down. "How could we lose him when he's hauling the Black behind him?"

"I-I meant something more drastic, Henry," Mr. Ramsay said quietly. "David pointed out to me that despite Alec having been so successful with his life, he's been under great strain a long, long time. Oh, I don't mean just the recent pressures, Henry, our need for more capital to operate the farm, all of which have added to the strain. It goes further back than that, David told me.

"He said we must realize what Alec has gone through since he first found the Black in that horrible shipwreck, which almost cost him his life. Then he had to spend all those months on that remote island until he was rescued. David said Alec's been through several traumas, and it was a wonder to him, as a medical man, that Alec has been able to cope with his life as he's done. It most certainly has not been any kind of a normal life for anybody, let alone a young man. Since he's had the Black, he's experienced one grim adventure after another."

"He seemed able to cope with his life to me," Henry said, "even enjoying it."

"David said it would appear so to anyone who didn't know. But there was tumoil within him."

"I thought his turmoil was his love for Pam," Henry said.

"No, Pam actually helped him. David told me that Alec's love for Pam was what he has needed all along. She was light and kind and happy, and she loved him very much."

"She was all that," Henry admitted.

"David said the truth of the matter is that Alec's capacity to love is greater than other people's, partly because of all he's been through and his *need* for a love as deep as his own."

"He's always had the Black and us," Henry said. "He knew he was loved."

The tall man smiled wanly. "It's different, Henry. You know that as well as I do, and with Pam he had a love that was very *special*. Her loss was more tragic to him than we can imagine. It may have triggered what David thinks could be a total collapse."

"So what does Dr. Warson think we should do?" Henry asked impatiently. "Sit still? Do nothing? Wait for him to come back?"

"Something on that order," Mr. Ramsay said gravely. "We can make quiet inquiries, but we can't notify the state police or the press and conduct a manhunt on a national scale. David is afraid that Alec is in deep shock and, perhaps, still deeper depression. If the police were to pursue him, and he became frantic, the results could be tragic."

"Tragic?" Henry repeated. "What do you mean?"

"Death," Mr. Ramsay said barely in a whisper. "Alec could be driven to believing that life isn't worth living without Pam."

Westward,
Ever Westward

6

The second day on the road, Alec set the pattern for the rest of the trip. He slept only after he had walked the Black in some unpopulated area. He would return to the truck, wrap his arms around the steering wheel and doze off, ready to leave again as soon as his eyes opened and he could see the road. He lost weight rapidly and his muscles, hardened by years of riding, started to become slack and weaker. Dark shadows blackened his eyes and the skin of his face was drawn tight by his illness. He looked gaunt and suddenly old, twice his age; his face that of one who was retreating from life.

"Pam is gone," he said leadenly. His voice was like nothing he'd ever heard before. It didn't matter. He really didn't care, and that was the trouble. Nothing mattered anymore.

Alec continued driving, sinking ever deeper into melancholy as the miles passed beneath the wheels of truck and trailer. He lost all track of time. There were moments when he struggled to come to terms with his terrible sadness, but such moments were only when he stopped the truck to see to the Black. The thought of food for himself revolted him but he had to feed his horse.

Mechanically, like a robot, he cared for the Black as he would have done during any of their more pleasant times on the road. Each stop he let his horse rest for thirty minutes, standing still in the trailer. He cut down the stallion's normal feed to one third, so there would be no possibility of "road founder." But he gave him all the hay he would eat, and he put electrolyte tablets in his water so any water during the long trip would be familiar to him. And whenever it was time to walk his horse, he was as careful as he would have been at home, the lead chain going through all three rings of his halter so he had full control of the great stallion.

When Alec drove on again, it was apparent, too, that the Black was kept somewhere in his tormented mind, for he slowed the truck at any kind of intersection and stopped and started slowly. But most of the time his mind was racked by horrible thoughts, and he could not rid himself of them.

With Pam gone there was nothing between him and the end of his life but empty time. Her youth reminded him that death was no mere jackal preying on the weak and defenseless. Nobody had been stronger and more alive than Pam. He felt she had been too locked into life to ever lose it. She had died as if her enthusiasm and joy for life had tempted fate—and she had lost.

Alec struggled again to come to grips with his mind, to think clearly, to see life as Pam saw it. Was it better to live one's life without ever running the risk of death? That was not to live at all. Did he himself not face death daily in his every ride at the racetrack? And would he have changed it? *No.* No more than Pam had done.

Alec called her name over the noise of the truck's engine. He was red-eyed, exhausted physically and emotionally, but his rational thoughts slowly helped him become a little calmer.

By the second night Alec was in the mountains of Georgia. Hunger finally made him stop when he saw the lights of a small restaurant ahead. He drove the truck to the back of it and went inside.

Alec ordered a bowl of soup and took it to a rear table. He ate as fast as he could, the spoon clattering against his teeth because he had no control over his hands. He got up and left the restaurant.

Hours later a northern snowstorm overtook him. The heater stopped working and he had to halt often to clear the ice from the windshield so he could see. All this he did automatically without thought of stopping and seeking shelter. He drove on, skidding on the icy road, but always pushing ahead, the powerful engine whirring down the mountainside. He didn't mind the cold of the cab. He felt nothing, nothing at all.

When daybreak came, the snow turned to a drizzling rain, and he hunched over the wheel, gunning the engine on the straight road. There was no traffic and his desire to move faster burned his brain.

The truck rolled down the coastal plain of Alabama, leaving the snow and dirty weather behind. He removed his goose-down jacket and felt the warmth of the southern sun on his body. He found a pair of sunglasses in the glove compartment and wondered why he'd ever left them there.

When night fell again, he stopped the truck to get out and walk the Black. Together in the darkness of wooded pines, they smelled the fragrant sweet odors of green grass and fresh manure. Somewhere in the area grazed cattle and horses. He heard the rush of a stream and led the Black toward it, taking deep breaths, trying to clear his head, to understand what he was doing and what was happening to him.

Reaching the stream, he removed his denim shirt while the Black drank beside him. The sound of a locomotive howling its way through the night reached him as he lowered his head into the swift, rushing waters, hoping their icy shock would revive him to the point where he could think straight again.

Back on the road, he leaned over the wheel and rolled on, traveling beneath the stars, knowing that somewhere beyond the swamps of Louisiana, the plains of Texas, he would find peace. Was it a vision of Pam he followed or the real girl? Where was he going anyway? He had no answer.

With the first streaks of daybreak, the landscape turned green and rolling. Soon afterward he reached a coastal highway, running along the blue waters of the Gulf of Mexico. He turned on the radio, and crazy, mad jazz flooded the cab. Then a disc jockey was telling him, *"Nothin', man, we got nothin' to worry about today! Jus' listen to my music, man, and live, man, live!"* Alec turned off the radio.

At dusk he passed the humming streets of downtown New Orleans, glad for the elevated highway that swept him swiftly through the city. It wasn't until he crossed the Mississippi River, its flooding, brown waters rolling down from mid-America, that he turned off the highway onto a narrow two-lane road.

In the purple darkness he drove past bayou villages where little children waved to him as they played. He didn't wave back. Getting away from people, even little people, was what he wanted. He wanted to see no one, no one at all.

He stopped once during the night, going into a small grocery store for gas and bread and cheese. No one bothered him. No one even noticed. He filled the gas tank himself and continued through a country turned strange and very dark. The road was elevated over Louisiana swampland, filled with inky water on both sides. There was no place for him to stop and rest.

He drove on through the night until dawn broke and ahead he saw huge structures in the dim light, oil tanks and refineries. He knew he was in Texas and drove ever faster, wanting to put the immense tanks behind him and smell the Texas cowtowns and ranches and manure that lay miles beyond.

Rain came upon him again by midmorning, splashing down in great torrents. But there were ranches on either side of the highway now, and men on horseback to prod him on his way, their ten-gallon hats and jackets dripping under the downpour. The truck slipped often, its wheels spinning in the mud, but he was always able to bring it under control again.

Across the Texas plains, he drove for several hundred miles. Westward, ever westward into the sun. The next day he crossed the border into New Mexico and saw the mountain peaks beyond. Was that where he needed to go? America's wilderness? All that was left for him was in the West, the great open spaces for a lonely man.

When night came again, he drove through the inky darkness, stopping only to care for his horse, then going on. All alone on the road, he had endless thoughts as he held the truck to the white center line. Where was he going? Would he find out? When?

By dawn the truck was zooming across Arizona deserts, great dry stretches leading north to the cliff towns of the Arizona mountains. Every bump in the road, every stretch of it, increased his longing for his Promised Land, wherever it was, *whatever* it was. The stones of old Indian ruins were all he saw on either side of the road. No people. No people at all.

Finally he turned off the state highway, again without question, and drove over a narrow gravel road that took him across a flat desert with ghostly shapes of yucca cactus on either side. It was wilder country than he'd known before. For a moment he closed his eyes in the heat of the sun coming through the windshield and pounded the wheel with his fists, uttering, *"Why? Why? Why?"*

Hours later he passed through a small Indian town, its streets full of holes. He slowed the truck while barefoot children watched him from the street and their families stood in doorways of dilapidated huts. No one waved or spoke to him as he carefully drove by.

On the outskirts of the town, burros walked with packs on their backs, their handlers usually straw-hatted old men with switch sticks in their hands. Only one spoke to him as he went by. "Where you go?"

Alec wished he knew. He bent over the wheel and went on, leaving the village behind.

Great mountains rose snow-capped in the distance, and he drove toward them, not knowing why but not questioning, not caring. Soon the truck began climbing, leaving the desert and gopher holes and cactus and mesquite behind. The air became cool as he drove ever upward through a narrow pass with sheer walls of stone on either side of him. He met nobody on the high road as the truck climbed until, finally, he reached a vast plateau at the top. Still beyond were the snow-capped peaks, but on either side of him were red mountainsides with long valleys.

Alec spent hours driving across the great plateau,

occasionally seeing strange Indians in tattered rags, walking along with knives hanging from their belts. But they paid little attention to him as he drove by, watching with no expression on their beaten, brown faces. He knew his own eyes were as empty as theirs. At last he had found people as lost as himself.

The road became rutty, making the truck and trailer bounce as never before. He slowed until he was barely moving, avoiding the ruts as much as he could, thinking of his horse.

At sunset he began climbing again into the heights of the mountain range before him. He passed another village as he climbed higher, the Indians wearing heavy shawls and watching him closely from under wide hat-brims. Some turned their eyes up to him as he passed close by, their eyes like hawks', their hands outstretched. Was it in friendship or for alms? He didn't know. Their world was dark, ancient and, he knew, where he'd wanted to be all along. How else had he found his way here?

Alec kept going, ever upward. The last rays of the sun were golden on the high peaks, and the air was keen and blue and cold. He stopped the truck to put on his warm goose-down jacket again. All that he knew of his world was far behind him now. What lay ahead? He didn't know. But soon, yes, very soon, he would have the answers to all his questions. His mind told him so.

In the jeweled, star-studded sky of early evening, he came to the end of the dirt road and stopped the truck. Stretched before him, between two mountain ranges, was another vast, arid plain. He felt the cold snap of night in the air as he gazed at the high plateau, which appeared to him as a great, empty sea. He was looking at a far, far country and yet it had a familiar, dreamlike quality. It was here he wanted to be. But *why*?

"All right," he told himself, "think. You must have answers."

He found he had none. His mind wandered between reality and a dream. What had brought him here was not real to him. Neither was his own self nor his own past. Half of himself had been left behind at Hopeful Farm and the other half was still ahead of him. He knew only that he wanted something and that he resented something. He resented what he had become and the cruelty of a world that had taken Pam from him.

Alec left the truck to care for his horse. Then, totally spent, he stretched out in the straw beside the great stallion. In the chilly dark he huddled in his warm jacket and hoped for sleep. At last he was far away from everything he had known except his horse.

In the dead silence of the night he felt the Black's warm breath on his face. It seemed to say to him, "Don't worry. Go to sleep. I'll look after you."

It was as if life flowed from the stallion's nostrils into his own tortured body and mind. For the first time Alec relaxed and felt safe. He began to go to sleep, really to sleep.

As It Was in the Beginning

7

Alec awakened and looked east into the sun. The morning light was intensely strong, all fine gold and flooding the dry earth. He turned to the high mountains in the west and they, too, seemed to be melting in the fierce rays of the rising sun.

His mind felt at peace for the first time, and he knew that this day was to be like no other. He had come to the end of the line, and perhaps that's what he had wanted all along.

With no thought of his own physical needs or well-being, he cared for his horse as he had done every other morning. Then, when the Black had finished his feed and water, Alec backed him out of the trailer.

Outside, the stallion stood quietly while Alec unsnapped the lead shank from the halter ring. Only the Black's eyes moved as the horse surveyed the seemingly endless miles of open land about him.

Alec removed the halter, dropping it and the lead shank to the ground; then he wrapped his arms around the stallion's neck, holding him tight as he had done so long ago on a lonely island. He wondered if this was what he had meant to do since he had left Hopeful Farm. Was this his answer—to go back to the way it had been at the very beginning? But to what end? For what purpose? To forget Pam, as if she had never been part of his life? *Was that his answer?*

Despite being free of halter and lead shank, the Black remained still, as quiet as the morning, proud and long-limbed and waiting. Finally Alec withdrew his arms from about the stallion's neck and looked at the pricked ears. His horse talked with his ears. They flicked east, and Alec knew it was in that direction they should go.

He felt the stallion's breath against his face as he stepped back beside the horse's head. Then he took two short, springy steps forward and swung his legs up while pulling on the mane at the same time. His body rolled and twisted in the air, reaching for seventeen hands of horse. Once astride, his balance secure, he turned the Black free!

The stallion's strides came swift and easy, and Alec moved with him as if riding him for the first time. Here he had no other existence. Here he could begin all over again. He cued the Black to greater speed, the horse running beautifully over ground that had known no other hoofs but his, galloping and putting more miles between them and the painful world they had left behind.

Alec rode with a fervor that he never had displayed on the racetrack, hurling himself and his horse into the vastness of the desert. He did not try to guide the stallion, but let him choose his own way. Swift and light, the Black ran in one direction after another, taking Alec through scrub and in and out of deep gullies. The great horse seemed to gather himself from time to time, changing direction at will, his excitement mounting as he felt no guiding hands, no control.

Alec's own excitement grew as he rode on. No machine could give this sense of motion, far greater than anything felt inside the fastest car or fastest plane. He rode a powerful horse whose heart drummed against his own, and he absorbed all the Black's energy and vitality into his own body, trying to forget his loss of Pam.

Alec screamed wildly into the wind, urging the Black on to still greater speed, more reckless than he had ever been, and knowing that his very wildness was creating problems he had never before faced with the black stallion.

Alec wrapped his muscular thighs about the Black, determined to stay on. He knew he would be thrown if he made but one mistake. Not that he cared what happened to him. If he was to be killed, he would be killed riding the Black. He welcomed the danger in order to forget everything he had known. But more than anything else, Alec was a professional horseman, and he adjusted his seat to a horse no longer his, but one gone wild with freedom.

The Black twisted and bucked. Alec felt the passion of the horse and gave in to his power. Instinct told him what the Black would do next, no matter how fast he did it.

The Black plunged and pawed for the sky. He ran into gullies, twisting among boulders and jumping over mesquite, his back kinked. He was forked lightning, streaking one way and then another. He stopped only to rear up on his hind legs and pitch straight down with his head between rigid forelegs. Then he bolted like the wind, rushing up gullies while Alec held on by iron knees and superb balance. Once in the open the stallion sprang forward, bucking and kicking and running, as if he had never felt a human on him before. Alec stayed on him, the lower half of his body like a vise about his horse, knowing he must never relax the hold of his legs or he was dead.

Alec felt as if his head were being jerked from his shoulders as the Black whirled on his hind legs. Then the stallion bolted and was on his way again. Alec tightened his legs on the body of live fire beneath him. His bones rattled and he felt the stinging lashes of the Black's mane against his face. They were like hot wires, searing his face until he felt he could no longer stand the pain. To escape it, he lowered his head farther down on the foamed neck of his horse.

Finally the Black ran straight and true, and Alec's heart beat high from the challenge he had faced and won, staying on the stallion, *his* stallion, gone wild. His body felt shaken to pieces. He had been frightened but wildly excited. That was the way he had wanted it, and the Black seemed to have known.

Alec felt the magnificent surge of power as the stallion stretched his long legs to their fullest extent. He lowered his hands on the wet, steaming neck and felt the desert wind sweep over him, furlong after furlong, as it might have on a racetrack. But he did not want to think of the racetrack ever again.

There was no sound but the rhythm of racing hoofs over the earth. The Black was running at full speed, all fire over the scorched, parched land. And Alec was one with him again, sharing the stallion's swiftness and strength as he raised and lowered his body to the racing strides of his horse.

Now that the Black was no longer fighting him, Alec was certain the stallion knew where he was going. His ears were pricked and his wet nostrils blown out. He had scented something. Only once did he stop to change direction, then resume his headlong flight. In another mile he came to a dead stop, head up, eyes surveying the land.

When the Black moved forward again, it was only at a slow gallop. Within a mile, Alec made out a brown pool in the rock outcroppings of the desert floor. It was a waterhole, and it was water that the Black had scented from far away. Only then did Alec realize how thirsty he was and what the water meant to both of them.

The stallion went directly to the pool and, lowering his head, swept away the brown scum that floated on top to reach the clearer water below.

Alec slipped off the stallion's back, breathing heavily. The wild ride had knocked him about so much that blood was running out of his mouth and nostrils. He fell to his knees, then flat on his stomach in the mud beside the pool. His clothes were torn to shreds. He lay still, in a deep state of exhaustion, his face in the torpid water.

As It Is Now

8

Moments later Alec lifted his head from the water to find the Black standing quietly beside him. The stallion had turned to the east, his ears cocked and wet nostrils blown out. Following his gaze, Alec saw what had attracted his attention. Something was coming from the east, creating a cloud of dust fuming from the earth. The cloud gradually grew larger until, finally, Alec could make out the shadowy figures of a large herd of horses racing toward them!

The Black's eyes followed the fast-moving herd, his body arched back against stiffened forelegs, his neck defiantly curved. Sweat poured from his body.

Rapidly the horses came closer, spread out in a line across the plateau. Alec recognized them as wild mustangs. Were they coming in from the desert to drink at the waterhole?

The huge herd slowed when they saw the black stallion and sniffed the wind for danger. Finally they halted. Alec saw only beauty in their wildness, their suspicions, their unbounded freedom. But, actually, their bodies were raw, rough, scrawny and knob-headed. Alec realized that it was only their dominant will to be free of all restraint that made them appear so beautiful to him.

They moved closer to the waterhole, tossing their heads high with nostrils dilated. The bright sun brought out details of prominent eyes, tapered noses, small bodies and slender legs. They came in all shapes and sizes. Their coats were of varied colors—brown, bay, sorrel, roan, dun, gray, white and paint—and covered with scars.

The mustangs came to an abrupt halt again, eyeing the black stallion and sniffing his scent. Suddenly they broke the stillness with loud snorts, wheeled and dashed away, speeding once more over the desert, an earth-skimming mass of horseflesh.

When the dust cleared, Alec saw that a few horses had stood their ground without fleeing. There were six mares, all with suckling colts at their sides. Just behind them were an old stallion, who looked too tired to run anymore, and two yearling colts who ran about as if undecided which to choose, freedom with the large herd or the chance to lead a small band of their own. Alec knew it was the water that had kept the mares behind, for they needed it more than the others if they were to continue nursing their foals.

They came closer to the waterhole, leaping and stomping, raising a cloud of dust around them as if that would conceal their presence. Alec watched them closely, for they seemed more playful than fearful. But they were cautious of the black stallion, circling downwind, the better to smell his odor.

One mare was more curious, more adventurous than the others, Alec saw. She was the only black in the small band, but as raw and rough as the others. What set her apart was a long, raven tail that reached to the ground and a foretop that fell to the tip of her nose. In order to see, she constantly tossed her knobby head, throwing the forelock back over her ears. Her interest in the Black set her apart as well.

She left the other mares, daring to come closer to the waterhole, quivers running along her flanks while she continued to toss her head in a series of impatient and coquettish jerks. Alec wondered if she had an affinity to stallions of her own color, for the foal at her side was black too. It happened sometimes, regardless how one explained it. The other mares were white, bay, roan and dun, and they all stayed put while the black mare moved ever closer to the black stallion. Her snorts were loud and startling, rolling over the desert, but they were not alarming, not the signal for flight.

The other mares seemed to want her decision as to whether or not it was safe to approach the waterhole. They stood still, waiting, while the two young yearling colts, who coveted the mares for their own, stood with them, too immature to assert themselves. The old stallion was far away and alone, no longer possessive of the mares; he was content to give way to the young stallions, whose vigor and aggressiveness he could no longer match. It was only a question of time before the yearling colts drove him away to become an outcast.

Alec knew this small group would rejoin the large herd as soon as their suckling foals could keep up with the others. Then the yearling colts would have to withstand combat with other stallions in order to maintain their monopoly on these mares. His eyes returned to the black mare, who was moving ever closer, still sniffing the wind but seemingly sensing no danger.

Alec rubbed his face, wiping the sweat from him. Perhaps the smell of him, so much a part of the Black, was the reason she scented no danger in his own presence. Perhaps she understood from the smell of him that he had the nature, even the mind of a horse. It did not seem odd to him at all that he was there, alone with wild horses.

The Black uttered a soft, muffled neigh and the black mare came forward eagerly at his call, followed quickly by the others. Reaching the water, they all drank deep, ignoring Alec. He watched them without moving so as not to frighten them. Some mares pawed and rolled in the muddy sides of the hole, and when they were done they came out of the water, full and logy, and stood still, waiting. It was as if they welcomed the Black as their new monarch.

The black mare circled about, tossing her mane and forelock the better to see the black stallion. She uttered raucous neighs, eyes sparkling with fire, implying that he should be well aware of the incredible honor that had befallen him by her attentions.

The Black tossed his head, sniffing the scent of his new harem. Within his great body was a wild, fierce, almost intolerable longing for a mate. He became more excited and gave a sudden, shrill neigh. Gathering himself, he rocked back on his hindquarters; then he plunged forward, running around the band at a powerful gallop that brought him back to the waterhole, scattering the mares and foals. He wheeled sideways to avoid the black mare, as though to tease her, then he sped off again without slowing his pace. The muffled and thunderous beat of his strides seemed to echo his exaltation, his renewal of life.

Alec watched him, knowing that this vast land with its wild horses made the Black act as he did because it was *his* way of life as well as theirs. His memory was fixed to what he had known long ago and now had found again. No longer did the Black have to dream of freedom; it was his for the taking.

The black mare had not scattered with the others. She stood alone, unafraid and waiting for the tall stallion to stop his vigorous display of leadership. Her eyes were bright and searching as her gaze followed him—and, for whatever reason, Alec saw his Pam in those wild eyes, so intense and curious, questioning and, above all else, *unafraid*. The mare snorted oc-

casionally, but the sound of it was almost musical—
and Alec thought of Pam's laughter, which meant to
one and all the love and joy of life itself.

Alec lowered his head and wept for the girl he had
lost.

The black stallion returned to stand beside the ex-
pectant black mare and continued his courtship of her.
He was ardent but without brutality as he nibbled at
her sides and neck, infecting her with his own maddened excitement. He rose to his full height, a gigantic
figure on his hind legs, striking the air with his forelegs
to maintain his balance, his long black mane waving
from his efforts. He was the picture of superb power,
his head stretched over the mare's neck, his nostrils
dilated, his eyes darting fire.

It was many moments later when Alec washed away
the tears that had racked his body. He went to the
Black and told him, "Go where you will. You have
done all you can for me."

Alec gave the Black a soft clap on his wet neck, and
it was the only signal the giant horse needed. He
trotted off to gather his small band together; then with
a mighty snort he wheeled and led them across the
desert.

In a state of shock over what he had done, Alec
watched them go, wild and free. The black mare raced
close beside his horse and Alec thought that it, too,
was the way it should be. The Black had found a mate,
but Alec had lost his. What was a man born for? To

find a mate, wasn't it? To have Pam, to make a home for her, to have children with her, was what Alec had wanted most of all. It didn't matter what happened to him now.

The Wild One

9

In the distance Alec saw the Black turn the small band and drive it back toward the waterhole. He tried to focus his mind on what he had done in setting the Black free. To what end? he asked himself. Nothing made sense to him. He no longer knew what he was doing and was acting on impulse only.

The black stallion drove the band across the desert, tolerating the two young stallions for a while by allowing them to race alongside. He punished any mare that lagged behind by ramming his head into her ribs or nipping her ear. Neither did he allow the foals to lag behind, prodding them to stay close to their dams. He turned them just before reaching the waterhole and sent them in the direction he wanted them to go, westward toward the high mountains.

Alec watched them leave, dazed, his mind drugged

by the desert and the solitude of his own making. He was desperate and alone. He knew no yesterdays or tomorrows. He had relinquished all desire to judge or act. His thoughts came only in splintered flashes. He knew he really had come to the end of the line this time.

The sun's rays glittered on the sandy gravel before him. He was content to die alone, knowing the Black was free to live as he pleased and no longer needed him. But somewhere in his chest sobs were heaving. There was no reason not to cry if he felt that way, he told himself. He could spend whatever time he had left in any way he chose. No one would know.

Alec watched the horses as they moved across the desert, more slowly now, for the foals were having a difficult time keeping up with the mares. Finally the black stallion brought them all to a halt to rest the foals.

Alec's eyes were fixed on the band as he drew a bare arm across his face, smelling not his own sweat but that of his horse. Ever since he was a small boy he had thought only of horses, even of *being* a horse. He had acted like a horse, run like a horse, neighed like a horse. "So maybe that's how it should end," he told himself.

Alec's eyes darkened as he saw himself as a wild and free mustang. His mind was taking a twisting, curious turn that he could not understand, but accepted.

Suddenly he began moving in the direction of the band, not knowing exactly what he was doing but not caring either. He felt strength returning with his exultance in a new way of life. A defiant look replaced the dazed redness in his eyes, a look similar to that of a young, unbroken horse. He strode faster over the ground until he had broken into a trot. Throwing back his head, he uttered loud, wavering neighs to the distant horses. Then he broke into a run, his muscular legs moving rhythmically, effortlessly.

The black stallion moved the band again, now traveling in a more northerly direction. He drove the group rather than led it, still punishing laggards, the young stallions as well as the mares and foals. He seemed to know exactly where he wanted them to go.

Alec called to him repeatedly from far behind. He felt new strength in his legs and was able to keep the horses in sight while pretending to be one of them. He raised his head high to sniff the wind as they did. He wanted them to see him, smell him, accept him. He wanted to be as wild and free as they were!

As time passed, Alec found that he could travel in sort of a trotting walk for a long while, breaking into a run whenever necessary to keep the band in view. He was proud of his endurance, his ability not to fall too far behind. And when the horses stopped to graze, he gained on them, wishing he too could live off whatever grass they found. So for a long while he was able to stay within sight of the wild horses and think of himself as one of them.

Far in the distance, too, Alec saw the dust clouds raised by the larger herd of mustangs and he knew the Black was on his way to join them. For what purpose? To enlarge his band? To make new conquests?

The Black moved his mares even slower because of the tiring foals. As the sun set behind the western mountains and twilight fell over the desert, Alec ran faster, hoping to reach his horse before the land was in complete darkness. Finally he realized he could not catch up to the Black in time, no more than he could have caught up to his own shadow.

Alec no longer felt the power of the wild life that had beckoned him so strongly and had given strength to his mind and body. Slowing to a tired walk, he began looking for anything to eat, anything at all. He combed the mesquite for beans and the cactus for buds or fruit. But he found nothing to sustain him and knew that it was only a question of time before he died of hunger and thirst. He had put off the end only a short while by acting out a childhood fantasy, believing he could be one of the wild ones.

He could no longer see the band, for the desert was dark and cold. Looking up at the ever brightening night sky, Alec stood still for a long while. A cool breeze swept across his forehead, and he found himself thinking of a night a few months ago when he'd watched Pam drive away in her car, looking forward to a trip to Europe from which she was never to return.

Alec recalled the words he'd said aloud in the night: *"Until she's back, the wind will be her fingers and her fingers the wind. And all space will be the smile of her."*

Alec remained still, his gaze on the stars, the desert wind on his face. He listened and waited until, finally, he believed with all his heart that he heard Pam's voice in the dead silence. It was as distinct as if she were next to him again, her body pressed close to his.

"Go on, Alec. It is not the way it should be. You must live. I love you. I am with you always, always . . ."

Then, with the wind caressing him, he felt Pam's hands upon him; life ran out of her fingers into his own tortured body. He peered into the night in a kind of fear, believing he was going insane. Or was it that his senses were so heightened by grief and fatigue that he was receptive to anything in the night air, anything at all?

When Alec moved, finally, it was not to follow the horses, for he was leaving them forever behind. Instead he made for the mountain range silhouetted against the night sky. There in the foothills he might find food and water to survive, as Pam had told him he must.

Alec walked in the middle of nowhere with not even a coyote breaking the silence. Life without Pam was a kind of doom, but something had finally stirred within him, something that was not just his but that he shared with Pam. He was not alone, not inside himself, even though he walked alone, without place or people. He would have to find his way to wherever his life led.

Hours later he fell down on the cold sand of the desert, exhausted. He fell asleep immediately, to awaken only once during the night when he thought he heard a loud nicker on the breeze from the north. *Maybe the Black misses me*, he thought. *Maybe he'll be back.*

The sun came up like a great ball of fire. Alec pulled himself to his feet and looked around. There was neither water nor grass, only cactus. To the southwest were the foothills of the mountains, his only chance to find water. He traveled slowly toward the hills, every step one of torture. His tongue became so swollen from thirst that it lay heavy and large in his mouth. He went on for a long while before he fell and could not get up. His gaze covered the great, empty sea between him and the hills he could not reach. It was a far, far country.

As he lay there exhausted, helpless in the sand, he thought of Pam's violent death in the car accident, so different than his own would be. He felt the first twinge of anger rising within him at the thought of such an ignoble death. His anger was deep-seated, a fathomless spring of slowly moving, invisible fire that prodded him into opening his heavy-lidded eyes.

Alec's mind as well as his body had been trained to survive in a world of steel-shod hoofs. He would not lie down and die. He was going to die *violently*, if at all. Clambering to his feet, he moved slowly toward the hills, one painful step at a time. His state of mind was somewhere between reality and a dream, but in his consciousness the anger remained. It was that which kept him going. It would not let him yield to death.

Before reaching the foothills, he became so exhausted that for a few seconds he lost consciousness. Yet his legs continued plodding until he reached the foothills and fell flat on his face. Even then he began crawling up the incline on hands and knees.

He knew that somewhere within the hills was water. Halfway up the incline, he reached a small hollow with overhanging cliffs throwing a few feet of shade over the ground. He crawled into the shadows, breathing heavily, grateful for the shelter from the sun.

It was not long before he moved on again, knowing there was no time to lose. He had to find water soon or he would die. He clawed his way on all fours up a steep path until he had reached the top of the hill. Looking down the other side, he saw a small green valley watered by a stream flowing from a spring in the rocks.

He wanted to cry out in joy but no sound came from his swollen mouth. Pitching forward, he rolled down the incline until his body came to a stop in deep grass. Still on all fours, like the animal he had become, he crawled to the stream and dropped his face in the water.

Boy Hunter

10

Alec emerged from dark unconsciousness hours later to find himself being rocked back and forth by rough hands on his shoulders. Turning his head, he looked into the black, shiny eyes of a young Indian squatting in the dirt beside him. The boy's body was as tense as a wildcat's, ready to pounce if Alec made the slightest effort to get away.

"Where do you come from?" the Indian asked. There was no sympathy, no compassion, in the boy's voice; nothing soft or warm-looking about his face. He sat quietly on his haunches, his hair straight and pitch black, pulled back and tied, with the front tucked under a sweated brow band. His face was flat and broad with a big nose, all as stony as his eyes. He wore a dirty gray shirt, blue jeans and bloodstained moccasins. He shifted his weight as he balanced a heavy backpack on his shoulders while repeating his question, "Where do you come from?"

Alec tried to speak out but couldn't. Again he felt the boy's strong hands on his shoulders, pulling him to a sitting position. He could now see a small herd of sheep grazing on the other side of the stream.

Forcing the words from his mouth, Alec said, "Please . . . I need your help."

The Indian's black eyes remained on Alec, still suspicious and a little wild. The boy appeared to be about twelve years old. Despite his youth he looked as if he was able to cope with anything. Finally the boy shrugged his shoulders and removed his backpack. Only then did Alec see the old shotgun lying on the ground beside him. Thinking the boy was reaching for it, Alec attempted to get to his feet.

Instead of reaching for the gun, the boy withdrew a can of warm soda from the backpack. Opening the can, he sipped from it. "You lost from the mining company?" he asked sullenly.

"I'm lost, but I'm not from any mining company," Alec said, the words coming easier now. He searched the boy's face for some sign of sympathy but found only bitterness. "Will you take me to your village?"

The boy grinned for the first time. "It's a long walk to our mesa," he said, lifting his moccasins to show Alec his bloodstained feet. "Are you with the Bureau?"

"Bureau? What bureau?"

"Indian Bureau."

"No, I'm not with the Indian Bureau."

"What are you doing here then? Are you looking for your loco brothers?"

Alec shook his head in dismay, and yet he knew that whatever happened between the two of them, it was far better than his being alone. "Who are they?" he asked.

The boy took a deep swallow of cola before answering. "They're up there, living on sacred ground," he said, nodding his dark head toward the mountains. "Mixed-up people, my old father says. Your people and my people, too, who cover their bodies with white powder. They drink. They get buzz on. They eat crazy weeds, jimson and peyote and nightshade, until they know nothing but a dream world."

"No, I'm not looking for them either," Alec said.

"Then *what* are you doing here?" the boy asked, his tone less hostile now.

Alec had no answer, not for the boy or for himself. "Please take me to your village," he pleaded. "I can walk . . ." He staggered to his feet, only to lose his balance and fall heavily to the ground.

"You're too weak to go anywhere," the boy said. Then, lifting the shotgun from the ground, he rested the stock on an elbow and put a shell in the breech. "I will shoot rabbit for us. Fresh meat is better to eat than pan bread and corn." He got to his feet and strode away, long and lean, like a young panther.

The boy hunter disappeared from view and Alec turned his gaze to the high country above, wondering if it was in that direction that he would find the Indian village. Up there the scrub gave way to tall trees, junipers, oaks and piñons. All were in shadow even though there were still several hours left of daylight.

To the east, the desert would still be glistening in the brilliant rays of the sun. Alec's horse was out there somewhere. Would he ever see him again?

It was an hour before the Indian boy returned, carrying a dead rabbit in his hand. He waved it in Alec's face but his eyes were on the eastern sky as he said, "Rain will come soon. We must move now."

With the boy's help, Alec got to his feet and together they walked to an overhanging cliff. Beneath the cliff was a small campsite, high enough on the valley wall to give a view of the desert. The site had obviously been used often, for ashes of other fires remained in a small pit.

Alec heard the coughing of thunder over the desert and looked toward it. Dark clouds climbed into the sky while lightning exploded within them like bombs.

The boy had a fire going, burning bits of tree bark from his backpack. He said nothing but his black, shiny eyes seldom left Alec.

A strong wind scurried ahead of the storm, meeting the cool air of the hills. The torrential rain would come soon.

The boy said, "Rain is good for our land. It brings water to the arroyos. Water is wealth in the hills."

From their campsite, Alec could see the sheep quietly grazing below. All was very peaceful despite the ominous blackness over the desert.

"What's your name?" Alec asked after a long silence.
"Alph."

"Mine's Alec."

The boy sipped from another can of cola, then abruptly offered it to Alec.

"Thanks," Alec said, taking the cola. Drinking it, he felt as if he'd been put into a new world where he had begun his life all over again.

The boy was watching Alec with his mouth wide open and grinning. Despite whatever suspicions he'd had at the beginning and the vast differences between them, it was evident to Alec that Alph wanted to talk to relieve his loneliness.

While they were eating their meal of cooked rabbit and tortillas, the boy said curtly, if not viciously, "All this land is ours. You do not belong here. You cannot take it from us."

"I don't want to take it from you."

"But your people do. They have big shovels digging up our mesas and canyons, taking our water."

"I have no part in it."

"Your people are killing us. My old father says so. He tells me everything about your oil, coal and gas companies. You destroy our grazing lands and leave us with nothing."

"They aren't *my* companies."

"My old father tells me about your federal courts, even the Indian Bureau, which cannot be trusted. I go to no bureau school. I tend my sheep and listen to my old father, who is the wisest of all."

"Your father is chief of the clan?"

"My *old* father is chief. He is the father of my father's father. He is the oldest of all. He knows all. He says this world will be destroyed because many of our own people are as bad as your people. They lease our land. They make tourist junk and sell it to your people. They are brown outside but white inside. They have gone over the edge into your world. They see only your dollars. We will live. They will die."

Exhausted from his long, angry tirade, the Indian boy stopped and sat back on his haunches, his eyes searching Alec's.

Alec said nothing. Such accusations were similar to those of the world he had left behind. Was it no different here?

Finally Alph spoke again, his voice more solemn than angry. "What has happened to the breed of white man?" he asked. "You take more from our land than you will ever need. You destroy the way it should be for all time. Why?"

Alec had no answer. "I don't know," he said. "There are many things I don't know about my people."

"My people were the first inhabitants of this land, but we do not see ourselves as masters of it," Alph said. "We are brothers to all who live on it, including our animal brothers. We take only what we need from this land."

"I know that," Alec said. If he'd ever seen a people in need, the Indians were it.

The Indian boy's speech became almost guttural as he continued, his words rising from deep in his throat.

"My old father has said that the time is not far off when we will be overcome by your people. But we still must not resist. We must have patience to await the One who will lead us to a safe place while the rest of the world is destroyed. There we will live peacefully with each other until it is time to emerge and help create a new world. My old father has said that only those who live by the laws of Creation will survive to start over again. We will be among them, for we are the Chosen People."

"And you believe all this?" Alec asked quietly. "It's a fearful prophecy."

"It will be as my old father says it will be," the Indian boy persisted, "and I will watch for the One who is coming. If he does not come during my lifetime, it will be during the time of my children or my children's children. It is only a question of waiting for him to come."

"How will you know him?" Alec asked, becoming intrigued by such a legend.

"I do not know what shape he will take but he will be riding the swift mount of Father Sun, a horse as black as the deepest blackness except for a small white spot in the center of his forehead. He will have great speed and magical powers. I will have no trouble recognizing such a horse."

Alec remained quiet when Alph had finished. He

thought of his own black horse, somewhere in the desert, a horse as symbolic to him as any supernatural horse would ever be to the Indians in their mythical tales and legends.

The boy stretched his long, thin legs before the fire. "Only the Chosen People will live," he said quietly. "It will be as my old father says."

"Will you take me to him?" Alec asked.

Alph shrugged his shoulders, and for the first time his eyes showed concern. "My old father has been gone from our village for many days," he said. "He may have gone to meet the Creator. I do not know."

Alec turned away, realizing he could only await the following day when he hoped the boy would show him the way to the Indian village. He had found much of the boy's story too difficult to understand. It bordered too much on mysticism, even the occult. Most of it, Alec decided, was the kind of folklore that had no place in the world as he knew it. All his rationalism tended to refute such a fearful prophecy as the end of one world and the emergence of the next.

They finished their meal as thunderheads climbed ever higher over the desert. Only a few drops of rain fell from the leaden sky; more rain would come when the bulk of the hot air reached the coolness of the mountains beyond.

As Alec watched the lightning jigsaw over the desert, he saw a flying, moving shape beneath the storm clouds. He blinked his eyes, trying to clear his vision to make certain he saw what he thought he saw.

As the clouds advanced toward him, so did the figure of a running horse. Jumping to his feet, Alec ran toward the desert shouting, *"Black, Black. Here I am!"*

Black Fire

11

The Black was only a short distance away from Alec, standing still on the hillside that led up from the desert. Alec found himself shaking, trembling. His eyes never left the stallion, and something within told him not to move, to let the Black come up to him of his own accord.

Even for so short a time, the Black had become accustomed to the wild. He was alone and free. Perhaps he remembered nothing of his domestic life of barns and farms or of Alec who loved him.

Suddenly the waiting was over. The Black gave a shrill neigh meant clearly for Alec. He gathered himself, rocked back on his hindquarters and plunged upward. The desert echoed to the wild pounding of his hoofs as he raced toward Alec, his black mane and long thick tail streaming in the wind.

Sobs came from Alec when the Black stopped before him. He threw his arms about the stallion's neck, and sounds and words flowed from his lips. He didn't know why the horse had returned, but he didn't need a reason. It was enough that the Black was here!

The Black held his head high, his eyes afire. Every line of his gigantic body trembled. That the Black had fought other stallions in the short time he'd been away from Alec was evident in his red-raw mouth and in the wounds that marked his black body. Some were jagged, made by cutting, ravaging teeth. Others were clean and straight, left by pounding, battering hoofs. Whether he had won or lost those battles made little difference to Alec. His horse had returned to him, and that was all that mattered.

Alec swept his hands over the wet, sweated body— the muscled withers, the great length of back, the chest and shoulders and legs. There were no serious injuries, and the flesh wounds would heal.

"Oh, Black," he said. "It's good . . . so good to have you back."

Alec reached out to the Black and touched the torn mouth. He uttered soft words in sympathy, and the stallion lowered his head, his large eyes alert but never shifting, never leaving Alec for a second.

Alec pushed back the long forelock. It was then he saw the wound in the center of the Black's forehead, a white circular spot where the coat hair had been swept clean, as a razorlike blow from a battering hoof might do. Luckily the blow had not landed square or the Black might well be dead. As it was, he would carry only a circular white scar, and in time the coat hair might even grow over it.

Alec continued to stand beside the stallion, his hand still holding the long forelock as if afraid to let go lest he lose the Black again. Suddenly the air became cold. A wind stirred, then mounted in intensity until it was whipping the stallion's mane and forelock. Alec looked skyward into the blackness of the storm overhead. It was time to seek cover at the campsite.

The rain came down in torrents, drenching and cold. Alec moved quickly to the stallion's side and, leaping high, he pulled himself face downward across the stallion's back. The Black whirled while he was still hanging on precariously, but Alec's hands found the thick mane and quickly he pulled himself upright as the Black came to a stop.

Alec spoke softly, a sound rather than a word, and the Black broke swiftly into a full run. Alec guided him up the incline and into the green valley. The triple, throbbing beat of the Black's hoofs over the hard ground came faster and louder, echoing the thunder that rolled overhead. Alec moved closer to the stallion's neck and adjusted himself to the rhythm of his horse. Through rain-blurred eyes, he saw that they had almost reached the campsite. Quickly he slowed the Black and brought him to a stop before the Indian boy who awaited them, his eyes wild with shock.

Sliding off the Black, Alec took the stallion into the

rocky shelter, which provided them with some protection from the storm.

"This is my horse," he told Alph. "He came back. I thought he was gone forever."

"You call him what you want," Alph said in reply. "I know him for what he foretells, *the coming of the end*." Lightning flashed overhead and thunder shattered the heavens.

Astonished by the boy's words, Alec asked, "What do you mean?"

"I have told you what my old father said. A horse of fire will come out of the desert, a horse as black as the deepest blackness except for a small white spot in the center of his forehead . . ." Alph's hand shook as he pointed to the stallion. "You see?"

Alec understood what the boy meant, for the Black's forelock was swept back and the white circular scar stood out glaringly against his black face.

"You're being silly, Alph," he said lightly, hoping to alleviate the boy's fears. "That's nothing but a scar he picked up fighting other stallions today. Look at the rest of him. He's covered with cuts."

The Indian boy shook his head vigorously. "It is as my old father has said it would be. He is the black horse of fire, and"—his eyes turned to Alec—"riding him will be the one who will lead us to safety."

Alec shook his head, more amused than alarmed. "Now you *are* being ridiculous," he said. "That's as crazy as you say your loco brothers are. I can't lead your people anywhere. It is you who must lead me.

Take me to your people tomorrow. They're older. They'll understand."

"Is that all you have to tell me?" Alph asked. "No more of what is to come?"

"There is no more to tell," Alec said, watching the boy's eyes fill with tears. "I'm sorry. Your elders will understand that my horse and I are not part of your prophecy."

The Indian boy backed away to the deepest reaches of the ledge without further word.

"Tomorrow we will go to them," Alec called reassuringly. "They will know that my horse is only a horse, and I am no different from you."

Later the drenching rain stopped as abruptly as it had come. The skies cleared and the night fell over the desert and mountains. The black stallion grazed a short distance away as Alec lay down on the hard ground of the campsite, trying to put his mind to rest and sleep. He couldn't see the Indian boy in the deep darkness of the ledge, but he knew he was there, somewhere. Alec hoped that by morning the boy would come to his senses.

The temperature dropped and the night became very cold. Alec turned on his back, moving his legs and arms to keep warm. The stars overhead were sharp and hard. Turning his gaze to the stream below, he could see the small herd of sheep congregating not far from the Black. Their eyes made tiny trails of light in the darkness.

Finally Alec fell into a deep, exhausted sleep. He

never knew that the Black visited him often during the night, his gigantic form silhouetted against the walls by the light of the small campfire. Neither did he know that in the wan grayness of early dawn, the Indian boy gathered his sheep together and drove them from the valley—vague, shadowy figures that climbed the hills toward the high mountains beyond.

The first rays of the morning sun fell on Alec's body, but it was not their warmth that awakened him. Instead it was the stallion's nose, pushing the back of his head. Without opening his eyes, Alec reached out to touch the Black's nostrils, warm and soft beneath his hands. The stallion made a gentle puff and pushed his damp nose harder against Alec's neck.

Rolling over, Alec said, "Okay, I'm up." He looked past the stallion to the valley below and realized the sheep were missing. He turned quickly to the far reaches of the campsite and saw that the boy was gone too!

Jumping to his feet, Alec swept the valley with his eyes. There was no sign of them. Alec guessed that Alph had left to alert his people to the coming of the black horse of fire and the fulfillment of their ancient prophecy.

Alec was on his own again. But this time he had the Black with him, and he could follow Alph's tracks to the Indian village. He felt rested and confident.

"Let's go, fellow," he said.

The Loco Brothers

12

Alec studied the valley for the first time in detail. There was another spring at the far end and enough good grazing land for a flock of sheep twice the size of the Indian boy's. No doubt the valley had been used over the years by many herders. At the far end Alec saw what looked like a trail leading from the floor of the valley up to the top of the cliffs. Mounting the Black, he rode toward it.

When he reached the trail, he knew it was the way the Indian boy had gone, for there were fresh sheep droppings. He was certain, too, that the trail had been man-made, for a stone embankment to prevent wash-outs ran up the near side.

Alec dismounted and led the Black up the trail. He climbed hurriedly, aware that the stones had been worn smooth by many feet before his own. At the top he found a high plain reaching to a series of wide ridges, one after another. Beyond them were the snow-capped mountains, and Alec knew that somewhere within them was the Indian village.

The plain was bleak and bare, the soil scarcely covering the rock beneath it. He found no tracks of the sheep, no droppings. But he knew it was in the direction of the distant hills that he should go. He mounted the Black and rode on.

When Alec entered the hills, the ground was soft beneath the Black's hoofs. Alec looked for the tracks and droppings he hoped to find, but there were none. There were many routes the Indian boy could have taken to reach his village and Alec felt the first signs of hopelessness.

He touched the Black's neck, sending him on. "We'll make it," he said. "Let's go."

Arroyos, flooded with rain from the night before, cut the land like dark ribbons before him. He rode around them, finding one rift in the hills after another, and coming ever closer to the mountains.

Alec climbed for a long time, finally reaching by midday the summit of the hills with the high mountains looming close by. Coming to a stop, he rested the Black and together they listened to the wind's muffled roar in the trees. Here the land was fertile and Alec would have looked for something to eat had it not been for the strange cry of the wind. It made him uncomfortable. The Black, too, was listening intently to it, his nostrils wide and flaring.

Finally Alec rode the Black forward, hoping to find a well-used trail or tracks, anything that might lead him to the Indian village. Despite the solitude of the high country, he could not escape the feeling that they were not alone. He stopped and shaded his eyes from the sun, trying to shake off the haunting feeling that there was danger ahead. He heard a distant wailing but he told himself it was the wind in the mountain canyons above. He stroked the Black's neck and rode on.

His mind was playing tricks on him, Alec decided. He had listened too intently to the Indian boy's talk of sacred ground and ancient prophecies. But if this truly was sacred ground to the Indians, there was something unholy, diabolic, about it as well. Otherwise he wouldn't feel as uneasy as he did.

Alec had gone only a short distance when he came to a great rift in the cliffs. At one time it had probably been the deep gorge of a river, long gone dry. There was the possibility that it led to higher ground, and he decided to risk traveling through it.

Alec rode up the gorge, the great crags of stone towering above him. Within a short distance the gorge widened dramatically, and Alec found himself in what he could think of only as a walled arena. The land ahead stretched for a half-mile or more between snow-capped mountains, and at the far end he could see a structure of some kind!

Alec stopped the Black dead in his tracks. At first he thought he might have reached the Indian village;

then he realized the structure was in ruins, an enormous pile of stone rubble. There was no sign of life anywhere, and yet Alec had a horrible, eerie feeling of being watched. A sense of chilliness, even dread, filled the air, warning him to be careful.

Alec looked at the cliffs above him. Up there the deep shadows gave a blurred appearance to everything his wild imagination could conjure.

Alec turned away. It was the utter desolation of the area that accounted for his fear, he decided. And the enormous pile of stone rubble in the distance, surrounded by this great waste of loneliness, only added to it.

Alec stroked the stallion's neck, more to calm himself than his horse. He told himself that he had nothing to fear while astride the Black. He had only to ride out of the area. He should not let his mind play tricks on him again. But despite his words of caution, Alec's gaze turned once more to the shadows in the rocky crags above, seeking answers.

Suddenly he knew that what he saw was *real* and no trick of his mind!

A ghostly body moved from behind nearby rocks, its grotesque arms stretched in his direction. The features were indistinct in the ghastly whiteness of its face, but it brutishness created a feeling in Alec of indescribable horror!

For a moment Alec sat absolutely still, paralyzed by what he saw. Then his eyes were drawn to other figures moving down the mountainside toward him. Suddenly

Alec realized that ghostly bodies were emerging from the shadows everywhere, a living, ghoulish mass of powdered blank faces. They seemed to grow by the hundreds as they made their way toward him!

It was only then that Alec recalled the Indian boy's warning: *"The loco brothers . . . your people and mine, strung out on crazy weeds . . . covering their bodies with white powder and living in a dream world of their own making."*

Alec tried to quiet his fears. The loco brothers were not monsters but people like himself. There might be some among them who would help him. He must look at them that way. He must not panic and try to get away.

Even though he recognized them for the human beings they were, many his own age, their bodies painted and powdered, he was filled with a terrible sense of overwhelming repugnance. He scrutinized the faces of those who stood just a short distance away from him, staring at him, wondering, perhaps, who he was astride such a horse. He might be as bewildering to them as they were to him.

The loco brothers stood just above him, balancing themselves suicidally on the edge of deep crags where one slip meant certain death. It was as though they had no fear of death . . . or didn't care, Alec decided. There was something about them, other than their ghoulish appearance, that suggested a state of life in death, something he could think of only as a deathless trance.

Suddenly Alec heard the swishing sound of a hurled weapon. The air close to his head was sliced, and a long spear landed a few feet away, its stone arrowhead imbedded in the ground!

Alec whirled the Black as rocks and arrows of every description were hurled at them. Riding low, he screamed into the stallion's ear and made for the entrance to the walled arena. But the loco brothers were there, too, lined up across the mouth of the gorge, mobs of them, their spears raised and waiting for him!

"Go, Black, Go!"

13

The black stallion bounded over the ground on long, slender legs, half on the earth, half in the air. Alec lay low on his horse's back, his eyes on the bulky grayish mass of human figures that blocked their exit from the walled arena.

"They mean to kill us, if they can," he warned himself as well as his horse.

A stone thrown from above struck the Black's head. He squealed in pain. A spear grazed Alec's shoulder and he heard shrieking voices as he lost his balance and almost fell.

The Black ran with fierce strides. Alec hoped that the very sight of the stallion would scatter those who awaited them at the gorge. Faster and faster the horse ran, his great nostrils puffed out in his fury. He held his long strides without a break, jumping over snags and boulders as if they weren't there.

At the gorge the pack of surging, ghastly heads and bodies came forward to meet the onrushing stallion. There seemed to be hundreds of them, and they showed no fear of the Black. Where had they all come from? Alec wondered. They were close enough now for him to make out the ornaments of bones, feathers and teeth they wore on their naked, painted bodies. Their heads were shaved, their eyes heavy-lidded and colorless. They moved toward him in a huge mass, twitching their bodies from side to side and gibbering in a maniacal, feverish chant.

The loco brothers opened their mouths in wild screams as the Black bore down upon them. Then, suddenly, they parted, scattering before the stallion's fierce onslaught. But they immediately turned to fling rocks, arrows and spears at the horse.

The Black screamed in rage and pain as the barrage of weapons fell upon him. He came to an abrupt stop and rose, pawing the air. A stone tore into the softness of his belly. He came down, shaking in his fury and undecided what to do.

Alec yelled into his ears, *"Go, Black, go!"*

The Black bolted forward, but it was not to escape the milling mass of ghastly figures. He reached out for the nearest one, grabbing him with savage teeth and lifting him from the ground. He shook him vigorously before flinging him back to earth.

Fire flashed in his eyes as he lashed out with steel-shod hoofs at others. Maddened with pain, he ran forward, then backward, as cunning and quick as a wild animal on the attack.

A rock struck Alec in the middle of his back and he cried out. His blood ran hot with rage as well as terror. He knew the Black was attacking to kill, and he would do nothing to stop him.

The Black moved into the milling throng of powdered bodies, his torn mouth spattering flecks of red foam upon them. He was determined to cut the attackers to pieces with slashing teeth and hoofs.

Now the ghastly figures were too close to use their weapons, so they resorted to clawing, hammering hands, seeking to pull the stallion down. Yet their eyes were fearful as the Black's striking forelegs caught one body after another, sending it to the ground.

There were just too many for the Black to fight. He was breathing heavily, blood spewing from his cut mouth. Alec turned the stallion in the direction of the distant ruins at the far end of the arena. He knew the gorge exit was closed to them and the only way to save himself and his horse was to outrun the horde of painted bodies.

The Black's hoofs struck out at those who attempted to stop him. They fell back, their screams filling the air.

Alec raced the Black up the long arena, knowing they could not stop to rest until they were well away from the crazed mob. He didn't know what lay beyond, only that there was no turning back.

As they approached the mass of fallen stones, Alec

brought the Black to a stop. The crumbling ruins had been a huge structure at one time. There was a portion that looked like an outer wall, thick and substantially built. But there would be no safety for Alec or his horse in this heap of rubble. It could provide them with cover for only a moment.

Alec slid off the stallion and moved his bloodstained hands over the Black's body, finding open wounds but no broken bones or torn tendons.

Straightening, he told his horse, "We've got to keep moving. They'll be following us."

Wrapping his arms around the stallion's foam-covered neck, Alec searched the area with his eyes, looking for a place to hide. Just beyond the ruins was a somber area of piñon trees with a snowy peak rising behind. As Alec made his way toward the trees, seeking cover, he realized that they grew in uniform rows. Apparently this land had once been cultivated.

Walking through the trees, Alec heard a distant sound—a low, booming roar. The Black heard it, too, for his ears were pitched in the direction of the sound.

Alec looked around, trying to pierce the dense cover to either side of him and find the source of the deep, continuous sound. Perhaps it would prove to be a way out of this madness.

Taking care, watching his horse's every stride, Alec broke through the bush. A moment later he came to a halt, staring in bewilderment at a crater-like pit from which the noise came.

Reaching the edge of the pit, Alec looked down into

the depths. The distant booming roar reverberated in his ears, but he also heard the distinct sound of a rushing torrent of water. It was then he knew that the sound came from an underground river.

His eyes turned to the far side of the pit where a path zigzagged down into the crater. Slabs of stone were piled high on the precipitous side to make a safe roadway. What purpose did the ancient inhabitants of this land have for entering the crater? Was it to fetch water from the underground river? Or was it to reach another way out of the walled arena?

A great upheaval of the earth accounted for the crater, Alec knew, but not for the man-made road leading to the depths below. It was wide enough for him and the Black to walk abreast with safety. But was there safety below? Should he go down it if the frenzied mob came after him again? What was his alternative? To fight them to the end? Or scramble up the high mountain just beyond the pit, exposed to their view and weapons?

As Alec looked into the crater, he felt a warm blast of air on his face. And with it he saw a flicker of light, a small crescent, burning for a moment in the darkness. What did the light mean? Where did it come from?

Suddenly Alec heard shrill screams behind him. Turning, he saw a sight that filled him once more with terror! A tightly packed mass of grotesque figures was moving through the trees toward him! He could see their powdered faces with eyes glaring at him.

A feeling of despair swept over Alec. He knew that
neither he nor the Black could face another fierce
onslaught and live! He scrambled to his feet as a shower
of stones was hurled at him. Leading the Black, he
ran to the far side of the crater and started down the
path.

Fire Below

14

The rock slabs piled high on the edge of the old road kept Alec and his horse from falling into the gigantic pit. Alec stopped once to look back up and saw the horde of powdered faces at the crater's rim. Those in front were on their knees while others pressed heavily against them, leaning over their comrades' shoulders, all stabbing down into the hole with long spears, striking again and again in futile attempts to reach him. Above the muted roar of the underground stream, Alec could hear the clang of their weapons against the stone.

It was only when they put up their spears and began hurling stones at him that Alec led the Black on. He hoped he wouldn't have to travel beyond the reach of daylight.

When they were safe from the hail of stones, Alec halted and looked up again. The loco brothers were still at the rim of the crater. At least they weren't following him, and Alec felt safe.

The crater and its noise might be taken for anything his pursuers cared to believe, he told himself. It might be enough to scare the crazed mob away and, if so, Alec was grateful for their ancient beliefs.

He remained where he was, wrapped in the semi-darkness of the pit, waiting for the loco brothers to leave and listening to their mutterings. He felt the Black's hot breath against his face and stroked the stallion's head, hoping his horse wouldn't go berserk in the confines of the crater.

The front rank of the mob was wavering, pushing back in fright at whatever it was they feared below. But those behind pressed forward, and a few bold ones made for the road down, their spears held high.

Alec felt a new surge of despair. *If they came down, what would he do?*

For a few minutes more he remained where he was, his eyes intent and watchful. Then, when he saw the braver ones making their way toward him, he plunged down the twisting road into the ever-darkening pit.

Finally Alec reached the bottom and came to a halt, believing he had gone far enough, that the loco brothers would never follow him so deep into the crater. The dull, heavy roar had become louder and it startled the Black. Alec touched him lightly, comforting him, trying to reassure him that despite the noise and the darkness everything was going to be all right.

Suddenly Alec felt the vibration of the floor beneath

him, and with it came a small flash of light! He realized immediately that what had been only a flicker of light when seen from above was, here below, bright enough to reveal a large underground chamber just beyond. In the dark again he walked quickly toward it, unmindful of danger, only grateful that he could periodically see where he was going. If he used his wits and did not panic, he might find another way out of the crater.

Within the chamber, submerged in the roaring sound, he waited until the light came again. Now he saw a high tunnel leading from the room. His hands reached for the Black and he felt the heat of the stallion's blood flow to him, giving him the courage to go on. He didn't know where the tunnel led but he would follow it, hoping it would lead to the world outside. Yet, as he made his way along, the floor of the tunnel sloped ever downward as if taking him to the very bowels of the earth.

The flashes of light grew in intensity, and Alec was able to see that the walls to either side of him looked hand-hewn. But he thought such a feat impossible. It was far more probable that some upheaval of nature had created this passage. But who knew the answers to this subterranean world with its unearthly light that came and went with ever-growing brightness?

The tunnel soon ended at a great arched entrance to another chamber, and it was from there that the greatest noise came. In the moments of light, Alec saw the underground river rushing through the chamber, the sound of it echoing and re-echoing against the walls, before plummeting into a pit to unknown depths.

Reaching the water, Alec found it icy cold. The Black was already drinking deeply and Alec lowered his body wearily and drank with him, hoping the water would relieve his hunger pangs as well as his thirst.

It was moments later when he noticed still another tunnel on the far side of the chamber. From it came a pale light that was interrupted by now-brilliant flashes.

Alec got to his feet and stood close to the Black. "Come on," he said softly.

He hurried through the chamber, finding his way in the gray, ghostly light. Entering the tunnel, he found it more narrow than the others. He walked until he left the noise from the stream behind and could hear only the sound of his own breathing and the ring of the Black's hoofs on stone.

The light was now coming in a pale, wavering cloud of luminous silver. He knew he was approaching its source, for he could feel a glowing warmth enveloping him. The blasts of air became warmer and stronger still, and the light grew more yellow in color.

Alec stopped, certain that he saw a ring of flame, boiling and glowing, just ahead. He watched it dim to nothing at all before bursting forth a moment later in a sudden flare of vivid fire!

Cautiously, Alec moved forward, one step at a time. He knew he had found the source of the light that had led him here. He entered a small room whose roof was much higher than any of the other chambers. In the center of the floor was a jagged hole from which the fire came. The murky glow above the hole brightened until it became a boiling caldron, glowing with an intensity that burned his eyes and caused him to turn away.

When the fire subsided, Alec stood in its glow, knowing he had nothing to fear from it. Indians might credit their gods for the fire below, but he knew that most everything he had seen in the area had been created by violent upheavals of the earth's surface. The whole area was one of faults in the earth's crust. A deposit of oil or coal below, burning close to the surface, could account for this fire.

Alec now had no doubt that he had entered the sacred underground world of an ancient people. The walls of the small room were covered with strange, fantastic carvings of Indian figures and faces, and to either side of the doorway across the room were immense pillars of hand-wrought stone.

He saw too that the way to the doorway had been worn smooth by many thousands of feet before his own. It was the only evidence Alec needed to believe that the doorway must lead to the world outside. He hurried toward it, hoping that soon he and his horse would be free again.

Alec had gone only a short distance before he stopped abruptly, thinking he heard something just beyond. He held his breath and listened. The sound came again, and he wondered if his ears were playing tricks on him. He could have sworn he heard a human voice, faint and distant. He remained still, his body shaking.

Slowly, cautiously, Alec went forward, aware that the floor beneath his feet was leveling off while the light ahead grew brighter. He walked faster as the tunnel widened, then swept upward to come to an end at a large opening.

Reaching the opening, Alec stood in shocked silence, unable to believe the sight before him.

He saw a great chamber, the size of a tremendous cathedral, oval-shaped and bathed in the golden rays of the late afternoon sun, which came through a long but narrow opening in the lofty heights above! But the sight that held him most spellbound was of numerous caves on the opposite walls.

A clear stream ran the full length of the chamber, and to either side of it grew moist green grass. The Black snorted at the sight of such lush pasture and moved toward it.

Alec wasn't aware that the stallion had left his side, for his searching gaze had found an aged Indian, very much alive, sitting cross-legged at a campsite. The old Indian held his arms outstretched toward Alec, looking at him with immense joy as well as sadness. Alec remained still, unable to believe what he heard.

"*I have been waiting for you all the years of my life,*" the old Indian said. "*You have come at last.*"

Chosen People

15

Alec remained where he was while the old Indian waved his gnarled hands at him, proclaiming in a deep, guttural voice, "Heaven has opened. Heaven has opened."

Alec was overwhelmed by the strange greeting. He stared at the Indian's dark, wrinkled face. He had never seen such sorrow written on a face before. The old man looked a hundred years old, his body frail, his long hair ghostly white and decorated with eagle feathers. Yet his small, powerful eyes were wild in what must have been his anticipation of Alec's coming.

Alec studied the old man's eyes, and he thought how much like the Indian boy's eyes they were. Was this Alph's *old father,* leader of the clan? If so, what was he doing here, deep in this subterranean chamber?

The old man continued to wave his thin arms toward Alec while repeating over and over again, "Heaven has opened. Heaven has opened."

Alec moved toward him, closer still. The Indian's body was naked except for a leather kilt and moccasins. Beneath taut skin, his bones showed prominently. He was sitting on the floor behind a line of blue-colored sand. Directly in front of him was a wood plank with bread, raw meat, tobacco and cornmeal. He gazed at Alec, his mouth open in what might have been a smile, showing rotten, decayed teeth. A feeble hand offered Alec the food.

The sight of the food drove Alec forward. He stepped over the line of blue sand and reached down for the bread. It was then he noticed that the old Indian's lap was also covered with blue sand. But more obvious, more sickening, were the bulging red sores he saw on the old man's bared shoulders and arms.

Alec took the bread but pulled back quickly, reeling from the stench of the wet and running sores on the Indian's body. He realized that the old man needed antibiotics, perhaps even surgery, if he was to live.

"How do we get out of here?" he asked softly. "You need help as much as I do. We're both running out of time."

The aged Indian nodded his head vigorously at Alec's words. "I know," he said. "Our wheel of life has finally turned full circle. We have seen the last full moon and the time is not far off when the end of our world is complete."

The light in the great chamber was changing colors as the sun's rays played upon varied layers of colored rock. In several hours it would be dark.

The Indian turned from Alec to look at the grazing stallion.

"Black Fire carries the sign of eternal life on his forehead," the old man said. "His coming and yours has been told since the beginning of time when the Blue Star first appeared in the heavens. I have lived to see you come."

Alec stopped gnawing on the bread and shook his head in dismay. It was the same prophecy he had heard from Alph.

"I knew of your coming, for I read of it in the plants and seeds as well as the heavens," the old man went on. "I saw the Blue Star explode. It was visible in daylight for twenty-three days before fading and seen at night for another six hundred and thirty-three days. That was the sign that your coming was at hand.

"The world as we know it will be destroyed," he said, "but you and Black Fire will lead those of us who are at peace with the Creator to the new world. My people will follow you, for we are all one, brothers. The others, those who have spread evil in the world, will be destroyed. We will create a new world under one power, that of the Creator."

When the old man had finished, Alec decided his only recourse was to humor him; otherwise he'd never get him out of the chamber and back to his village.

"Where are we now?" he asked.

"We are in the sacred pueblo of the old people, the dead ones," the old Indian said.

Alec looked up at the high walls with the great arched caves. Rock writings and colorful paintings were at every entrance, as well as ghostly handprints etched in stone. What had they meant to the families who once lived in those rooms?

"You must lead my people here," the old man said. "They will follow only you, for you have come out of the desert riding the horse of black fire at the time of the exploding Blue Star."

Alec shook his head more in sadness than bewilderment. The old Indian was senile and attempting to live out the prophecies of his ancient people.

"I'm not the one you've been waiting for, old man," Alec said finally. "I'm only lost, the same as you seem to be, but in another way. I can't lead your people anywhere."

The Indian ignored Alec's words, and his gaze turned to the black stallion again. His eyes, like his voice, were gentle when he spoke. "The horse of black fire possesses extraordinary powers. He is the extension of you. We understand that all things are the works of the Great Spirit. He is within all things—the trees, the grasses, the rivers and all the four-legged animals. We understand all this in our hearts deeply. My people will follow you to the beginning of the new world."

"Where are your people?" Alec asked. "How do we reach them?" All he could hope for at this time was to direct the old man's mind to returning to his village.

The old Indian lowered his head as if brooding or almost asleep. Alec waited, not wanting to prod him for fear he would talk of other things. He looked at the man's frail body with its chronic running sores. The colorful eagle feathers in his headdress couldn't offset the man's wretched condition and his immediate need for medical attention. If the old one remained here, his only destiny was death.

The old man muttered something in his sleep. Alec placed a hand on a bare shoulder, gently shaking him. "You're dreaming, old man. Wake up. It's time to go."

The Indian raised his head but made no attempt to get to his feet. Instead he met Alec's gaze, his small, piercing eyes clear and untroubled. He found strength from somewhere within his frail body to speak loud and clear of ancient gods, as sacred to him as was the Bible to Alec. He recited strange myths of a primitive tribe. The messages were of peace, and of belief in the fullness of life if one followed the laws of nature and universal brotherhood.

"It is all told in symbols passed from clan to clan from ancient times, symbols engraved in stone," he said. The old man made a great effort to raise his arms toward the images behind him and failed utterly. Exhausted by his long speech, he let his head fall once more to his chest.

When the old man spoke again, his voice was very low. Alec could make out only some of the words. The Indian was speaking of invisible spirits and the three worlds that had gone before and been destroyed as the present one would be.

Alec knew he could rationalize what he was listening to as nothing but the folklore of a tribe who had no relationship to the world in which he lived. And yet the old man was speaking of many things that were partly responsible for Alec's being there—a false set of values that seemed to dominate Alec's world . . . a world in which time and time again conflict threatened not only between nations but between peoples of the world, red, yellow, white, black and brown.

The old man raised his head once more to look at Alec, and when he spoke his voice was but a whisper. "This world will end soon or you would not have come. I do not know how it will be destroyed. It may be by raining fire or by spinning off into endless space. Perhaps the great waters will be loosened to cover the land. Or . . ." He paused, thinking for a few moments before going on. ". . . it could be by mankind's own hands with his own weapons. There will be no shelter for the evil ones," he warned, his voice rising. "Only those who are at peace in their hearts will be saved to take part in the new world to come."

The old man held Alec's attention through the long, lonely dialogue. Thinking of Pam, Alec said quietly, "I know what it means to despair and seek help. But I can't think of it as the end. Where will your people find safety, if what you say is true?"

"Their shelter is here in this sacred place. It was told to me by my father and fathers before him, all the wise and ancient ones from the beginning of time.

Here my people will be safe to await the coming of the next world. You must go to them and bring them to this shelter. They will follow you and Black Fire. You must hurry. Go now!"

"Why me and not you?" Alec asked, knowing he could not find his way alone.

"They await only *you*, for your coming has been told in the stars."

Alec wanted to shout, "You're crazy, old man, crazy!" But he couldn't, not with so much sorrow showing in the old man's eyes.

"You go with me," he pleaded.

"I cannot," the old Indian answered. "I am too spent with years of waiting. I have lived only long enough to set eyes on you." His eyelids closed and there was a sudden slump of his body. The eagle feathers on his headdress touched the ground and the blue sand cascaded from his lap.

Alec went quickly to him and held his frail body upright, unmindful of the stench that filled his nostrils from the sores.

The Indian's eyes opened, glazed and staring at Alec. His voice was only a creaking whisper as he said, "Go now. It is time . . ."

"How do I get there?" Alec asked urgently, gently shaking the old man's shoulders, trying to keep him conscious. "Which way do I go? Tell me."

"You know," the Indian said. "River Run . . ."

"*River Run?*" Alec repeated.

The frail body in Alec's arms collapsed totally. The

thin wrist he held became cold. Alec felt no pulse, no heartbeat at all.

The old Indian's eyes still gazed at him, eyes as sad in death as in life. Alec closed the lids over them. He continued holding the old man for many minutes more, repeating again and again for reasons he was not aware, *"Chosen People, Hopeless People . . ."*

River Run

16

The old man's body was so light that Alec had no trouble carrying it to the high sandstone wall. The cliff dwellings above, where most of the Indian's ancient ancestors had lived, would make a fitting place for his body, at least until Alec was able to reach others who might wish to bury him elsewhere.

The rust-colored wall above Alec looked like a stage setting and, for a moment, he thought he was acting in some kind of an amateur play. There was no reality to what he was doing at all. But he was not playing a part on stage. What he was doing *was* real, and a matter of life and death to him. He had to find a way out or, as it was for the old man, this place would be his tomb too.

The path leading to the first-story dwellings was well worn and Alec carried his burden to the nearest one.

He entered the cave with the old man in his arms, looking at the ancient drawings and symbols on the walls and wondering what they had meant to those who lived there so long ago. Then, carefully, he placed the old man upon the floor, the fine dust swirling about his frail body.

A few minutes later Alec returned to the Indian's campsite and put what was left of the old man's food in his pockets. Then he looked about, wondering which way to go. There was no more than an hour or two left of daylight.

Alec watched the Black move quickly in the dim light as he found one patch of grass after another to his liking, but often, too, he turned to look in Alec's direction, his eyes bright and ears pricked. He seemed interested in everything about him and unafraid.

Alec shook his head in wonder; it was as if his horse were in a paddock at home, not deep within this underground world. Alec wished he could feel the same way.

What had the old Indian meant when he'd said *"River Run . . . River Run"*? Alec wondered.

His eyes followed the swift rushing stream to the far end of the pueblo, where it swept through a narrow chasm amidst towering walls. Was there any way to follow that torrent of water to the outside world? Was that what the old Indian had meant by *"River Run"*?

Alec decided to use whatever daylight was left to find out. He followed the stream, looking for any sign of a trail that would indicate the Indian's route. The old man had been too feeble to travel far, so his village couldn't be far away. And yet Alec knew that the old man had been driven to reach the sacred pueblo by incredible determination, which could have taken him farther than expected of so frail a body.

At first the stream was shallow and Alec was able to cross it often as he made his way to the far end of the pueblo. The Black left his grazing to move alongside Alec and then surge ahead. Alec let him go, knowing that the stallion's instincts were far better than his own and that the Black might find a trail where he couldn't.

He saw the stallion stop occasionally to step around certain areas of the stream. When Alec reached them he found pockets of quicksand and became more careful, keeping closer to the banks. The flow of water became ever faster as he neared the narrow chasm ahead.

Finally Alec came to a halt. Ahead, sheer sandstone walls rose to either side of the torrent of rushing white water. He knew there was no way for him and his horse to go through such turbulence into the chasm.

River Run. Was this it? Alec wondered. But the old Indian could not have navigated the turbulent waters any more than he could. There had to be another way out besides the tunnel he had entered by. Where was it?

Alec looked around, knowing the ancient inhabitants of the pueblo had been protected from the elements outside by its great walls, and the stream had provided them with grass for their livestock and fertile soil to grow their food. But there was no doubt in his mind that they had had more than one entrance to the pueblo. Another tunnel had to lead to the outside world. He had only to find it.

Moving carefully in the shadows of the overhanging walls, Alec began to explore the banks of the stream for the start of a trail. He stopped when he came upon a low slab of rock with an Indian symbol etched on it. Parting the heavy brush above it, he saw a worn trail leading into a small but deep ravine!

Excitedly, his gaze followed the ravine as it dropped steeply toward the sandstone wall, coming to an end at the entrance to a large tunnel. He couldn't restrain the cry that came from him, believing he had found the way out!

The trail was easily accessible from the stream. Alec called to the Black to follow him as he broke through the brush and started down the ravine.

Great heaps of stone were piled everywhere, appearing as though the way had been cleared by hand. Alec could readily believe that at one time the ravine had been the original bed of the stream, and the ancient inhabitants had diverted the flow of water from this route to go through the chasm. For what purpose? To close the chasm to outside invasion, making the pueblo more secure?

Reaching the tunnel at the bottom of the ravine, Alec saw that its entrance was supported by great blocks of hand-hewn masonry. From behind, the Black snorted and Alec turned to him. The stallion's nostrils were flared wildly, sniffing unfamiliar scents. Alec reached out to him and the Black nuzzled his hand before shattering the confines of the ravine with a shrill blast.

"Wait here," Alec told him, stepping inside the tunnel entrance. He found himself in a tall chamber, dimly lit by daylight coming through a hole where the roof had fallen in. Stone and mortar were scattered about, and Alec knew that an earthquake or an underground explosion of some kind had accounted for the general disorder of the chamber.

The tunnel leading from the chamber was black as pitch. Alec went to it, undecided what to do. Had the old Indian found his way through it with the aid of a light? Alec looked around the floor and found a blackened torch. Picking it up, he found it faintly warm to his touch and knew he had his answer. The tunnel led to the outside world.

Alec returned to the entrance and sat down on the rocky floor, his eyes on his horse. He could get a fresh torch from the old Indian's campfire, which probably still burned, and find his way through the tunnel. But the Black would not be able to go with him, for the tunnel was too low, too narrow for a horse.

There must be another way, he decided, for the ancient inhabitants too had livestock. How had they entered the pueblo? He would have to find the way; he was not going to leave without his horse.

Alec was getting to his feet when he saw a large ring directly beneath the Black's hind legs. He went to it and swept away a thin coating of what looked like volcanic ash. Taking hold of the ring with both hands, Alec pulled. He was surprised how little strength it took to lift a large section of what was not stone but mortar. Putting it aside, he could see only empty blackness below. Then, bending over the hole and listening closely, he could hear the sound of rushing water. The sound grew louder and suddenly he realized the water below was rising to the surface in the form of steam!

This was an area, he guessed, where faults in the earth's surface allowed molten rock to seep close to the surface and heat underground water. Whatever he had done by uncovering the hole had resulted in some underground pressure wave, turning the surface water to steam with the high temperature.

Alec was attempting to put the slab of masonry back over the hole when he heard what sounded like an explosion at the top of the ravine. It startled him and he leaped to his feet. The sight that met his eyes was even more startling, for a rush of water filled the trail above and was cascading down the incline toward him!

Alec knew it had to be water from the stream, but what had diverted its course? Had his uncapping the hole created an underground pressure wave so great that it had triggered a landslip above? Had the ancient ones planned this too?

Shocked to the point of immobility, Alec watched the first rush of water reach the bottom of the ravine and pour into the hole, steam rising in its wake. Only when the water deepened around his legs, tearing at his balance, did he realize his danger. The water was increasing in volume and speed and would soon fill the whole ravine, making it impossible for him and the Black to leave!

"Get out of here!" he shouted to his horse.

The water was churning over his knees as Alec plunged up the narrow ravine. He lost his footing and grabbed hold of the stallion's mane for support. Half-way up the ravine, the water was to Alec's waist as the Black tried to resist the force of the ever-increasing current.

Alec lost his hold on the Black's mane and the water cascaded over his head, the current seeking to hurl him back toward the gaping hole. Reaching out, Alec caught hold of the stallion's tail and held on to it for his life.

The Black plunged forward, trying to stay on his feet, but the rush of water seemed too strong for him too. He lost his balance and his hoofs flayed the water as he tried desperately to regain his footing. Finally he stood upright again and once more fought the raging current. Step by step, he struggled up the ravine.

Alec kept holding the stallion's tail, knowing they were nearing the upper part of the ravine where the current was less strong. He managed to get his feet under him and struggled forward with his horse.

Only when they had reached a point above where the stream plunged into the ravine did Alec know they were safe. Where the ledge with its Indian symbol had been was now only a deep rift in the bank through which the stream flowed. What had caused the land-slip? What explosive force had he triggered from below?

Exhausted from his grim fight with death, Alec let go of his horse and lay still.

Hopeless People

17

Alec rested a long while. Then, feeling that his strength had returned sufficiently to allow him to go on, he got to his feet.

The stream was still pouring down into the ravine through the rift in the bank, its waters forming a huge whirlpool over the hole he had uncovered. It was only when his gaze returned to the chasm beyond that he fully realized what had happened.

Now that the stream no longer flowed through the original bed, the chasm was a ragged, stone-laden trail through the sandstone walls!

Calling to the Black, Alec made his way quickly to the chasm. The streambed rocks, slippery with slime and mud, were the only obstacles he had to face to leave the pueblo forever behind him! He chose his way slowly, leading the Black, well aware of the danger of breaking a leg.

Within minutes the chasm widened and the way became easier. Alec increased his pace, anxious to find out where the dry streambed led before dark. To either side of him he made out more caves in the high sandstone walls, all staring at him as if they were black eyes watching his progress through the chasm.

The chasm widened into a large canyon, bright in the late rays of the sun. Alec stopped to rest, a ball of sweat running from his face. He hoped he could find the Indian village before his food ran out. Above the canyon walls, he watched vultures spiraling down a thermal. They were the first signs of life he'd seen outside the pueblo. Alec got to his feet, determined that he and his horse would not provide food for such scavengers.

The ground over which Alec walked became a wasteland of black shale and other rock. Finally he emerged from a narrow passage in the canyon walls to find a broad plain stretched before him. The flat-topped plateau appeared to be open country, seemingly devoid of all life from where he stood. The light of the setting sun was intensely strong, flooding the dry earth with an overwhelming golden glow. Somewhere on the plateau, Alec believed, he would find the Indian village.

Alec mounted the Black and wrapped his arms about the stallion's neck. Despite the growing coolness of the air, he felt sweat pouring down between his shoulder blades. For several miles he rode seeing no sign of life. But suddenly the Black's ears pricked forward and he neighed shrilly. Only then did Alec notice the wisps of smoke that were beginning to rise in the north. He watched the spirals curling ever higher into the sky, his first evidence of human life!

Alec galloped the Black for a full mile before slowing him to a walk. They were nearing a sandstone cliff about forty feet high, rising like a small rock fortress.

A well-traveled trail led to the top of the cliff and as Alec rode up it he heard the bleating of sheep beyond. When he reached the end of the trail, he found that the cliff was sheared cleanly at the top. Stretched before him was a small mesa of flat tableland, one of meadows and plowed fields! At the far end were humpy shacks and distant figures of people moving between them. Closer still was a crudely fenced area holding a flock of bleating sheep.

As Alec neared the sheep, a shaggy dog lying in the dust leaped to his feet and began barking. From behind the rocks an Indian boy emerged, one who wore a red rag around his head and whose face Alec readily recognized.

"I have told my people of your coming," Alph said, his voice disclosing no surprise at Alec's appearance. "It is as my old father has said it would be."

"Your old father is dead."

"He is not dead," the boy answered. "I am told that he sleeps with the ancient ones in the sacred pueblo. Now you and the Black Fire will take us there too, so we will be safe and live to help create the Fifth World."

"I'm not going back," Alec said. "But what's to stop you and your people from going, if that's what you want?"

"It is sacred ground. We can only follow you and the black horse of fire. It is so written in the stars."

Saying no more, the Indian boy ran off toward the village, the shaggy dog barking at his heels.

Alec rode the Black into the village, a long row of decaying adobe structures with shuttered windows, shacks of boards and dirt and outhouses set amidst concrete rubble. His eyes greeted the women and old men who stretched out their arms to him in friendship and welcome. And there were children too—lots of children—who gleefully sought to reach up and touch the black stallion. Where were the younger men, the fathers of these children? Alec wondered.

Alph called, and when Alec rode forward he saw the elders in the tribe spreading lines of blue sand before the Black's hoofs, as the old man had done in the underground pueblo.

Alph stood beside a tall, lean woman. "This is my mother, Cloud Dancer," he said.

The woman smiled while speaking to Alec in her native tongue. Alec realized she was not as old as she looked, and at one time had been very beautiful. But now her face, like her body, was shrunken and lined with fatigue.

"She welcomes you to our house," the boy interpreted. "You will stay with us until it is time to leave. My father hunts with others of our clan but they will return soon now that the sun has gone to rest." His brown face suddenly showed concern. "We have time to wait for them?" he asked.

Alec nodded. "We have plenty of time," he said. Then he turned to the crowd gathered around him. "Is one of them your chief?" he asked the boy. "I would like to talk to him."

"We have no chief," Alph answered. "Only wise old people. But it is my father who will speak with you. He will do what needs to be done."

"Then your father will understand what I have to say," Alec said hopefully.

"We have corn for Black Fire," the boy went on eagerly. "He will be fed well before his journey."

"That's good." But Alec believed with all his heart that *nothing* would get him back into that underground world he had left behind.

Later, with the Black fed and safe within a small fenced corral close by, where he could be watched, Alec followed the boy to his home. It was a lean-to shack with odd pieces of wood nailed together and the crevices sealed with black plastic.

Alec went inside to find the interior dark and cold after the lingering bright light outside. There was only one room and it was dimly lit by a kerosene lamp standing in the center of a wooden table. In the corner of the room was an empty oil drum used as a wood stove for cooking and warmth. Spread over the floor were sheepskins for beds. The boy's mother stood at a sink washing pottery dishes she removed from a cupboard above it.

Alec watched the woman grind corn and make it into a mush before wrapping it in cornhusks. Then she put the husks in hot ashes, covering them with leaves and sand while building a small fire over them.

Later she called them to the table, setting down a pitcher of thin milk and filling their glasses. Alec found the steaming food delicious. He didn't know if it was as good as it tasted or if his hunger made it seem so. It didn't matter. He ate until he could hold no more and felt strangely content.

Afterward Alec went outside to stand in the swiftly falling night, wondering how he could change these people's minds about him and obtain their help. When the men returned, he would tell them that there was no need to go to the sacred pueblo. They could see that the world was *not* coming to an end, despite their fearful prophecy.

The first stars were beginning to appear in the night sky. Alec never had seen them so bright and numerous, and he accounted the clear air and altitude of the mesa for it. The Indians read their prophecies in the stars. He looked for the Blue Star the old man had mentioned but couldn't find it.

"I saw the Blue Star explode," the Indian had said. *"It was visible in daylight for twenty-three days before*

fading and seen at night for another six hundred and thirty-three days. That was the sign that your coming was at hand."

It was all just a figment of the old man's imagination, Alec decided.

The air was cold and hard to breathe; yet Alec didn't want to go inside. He stretched and shook himself. Then he turned to the stars again.

It was so easy, he decided, to lose oneself in legends as did the Indians. And so seductive. The Indians and their gods, all written in the night sky. And yet, he reminded himself, this clan had not retreated from life but had waited patiently for whatever it was they believed in. It was more than he could say for many of his own people, including himself. He had thought his own world was coming to an end with the death of Pam and had run from it.

Alec listened to the voices of the mesa. Some were familiar, some not. And there were cries he wondered if he heard at all. The land was playing tricks on his ears, as had happened to him before. Nevertheless, he was beginning to believe in many new things, things he had learned from this land and its people within a very short time.

Alec heard the murmur of voices coming from the decrepit shacks and the sound of meals being cooked and eaten. Lamps shone as small squares of light in the darkness. But Alec was aware of the squalor inside each shack, and he could not think of them as being warm and homey.

Like many others, who had read schoolbooks and stories, he had thought the lives of Indians were bright and colorful, as beautiful as the jewelry they made, as colorful as their paintings and ceremonies. Instead he had found them in poverty and sickness, living on scrubland, sweating all day to cultivate enough food to eat, and freezing at night in dilapidated shacks, clothed in rags and sleeping on dirt floors. Actually, from what he had seen they were not the chosen people at all, but among the most hopeless people on earth.

The cold wind raced across the mesa, carrying the Black's sharp whistle and the sound of footsteps in the darkness. The hunters had returned and Alec went forward to meet them.

The Blue Star

18

As Alec neared the Black's corral, he heard whispers and the soft padding of human feet. Finally he could distinguish the faces of several men standing by the fence, looking at the Black who, strangely, stood still.

The tallest of the men strode toward Alec, his arms raised as if they were wings.

"Our world is doomed, but even the doom is one of splendor," the Indian said, his voice carrying a sense of joy as well as proclamation. "This night is not the night of the white man's world," he continued, his gaze turning upward. "This is not the sky of his race. The god in this fire is huger than the white man can understand."

The Indian's long arms descended to grasp Alec by the shoulders. "You have come with Black Fire to lead us to the Fifth World as our old father has said. We are ready. You have only to guide us."

Alec shook his head in dismay. "I can't lead you anywhere," he said. "I'm not what you think I am. I'm lost. I've been sick. I'm trying to find my way back home."

"None are lost who follow Black Fire," the Indian said. "It is he who will guide us to the Fifth World, for he has come from the foot of the sky. He is the horse of Father Sun and carries the sign of eternal life on his forehead."

Taking a black eagle feather from his headband, the Indian kneeled down and quickly tied it to the near front leg of the stallion. "His body is like an eagle-plumed arrow," he went on, looking wondrously at the horse. "His tail is a trailing black cloud. His ears are the crescent moon. He has the power to see both day and night, for the big stars that sparkle are his eyes. From his nostrils come bolts of lightning."

The Indian turned from the Black to look at the night sky and proclaim, "He will lead us to the sacred pueblo, for the end of the world, as we know it, is upon us."

Following the man's gaze, Alec saw what looked like a small comet on the far horizon, a faint trail of blue gases streaming behind it.

The Indian then fixed his eyes on Alec and asked, "Do we leave this night?"

Alec's voice trembled as he answered, "Not to-night . . . tomorrow, maybe tomorrow." He hoped by then he would have thought of something to avoid returning to that underground world.

Later that night Alec lay on one of the sheepskin beds in Alph's house trying to decide what, if anything, he could do. He had no solution and, finally exhausted, he allowed himself to fall asleep.

Alec had no idea how long he'd slept when he awoke and sat upright. He looked at the sleeping figures of Alph's family and had a puzzled sense that something unusual was about to happen. There was a misty look about the shack; then, slowly, a soft white light began to glow in the room.

At first Alec thought the flame from the lamp had been left burning. But he saw that the lamp was out. He found that he could see each piece of furniture but in a strangely unreal way. He looked again at the lamp. It was definitely out and yet the room was now filled with a soft but luminous light.

An intense stillness prevailed until suddenly he became conscious of a faint, continuous sound, almost that of a soft voice speaking to him. He listened intently. With electrifying swiftness, old days he had tried to forget sped before his eyes, and old wounds, which had not healed, opened. Then he was looking into Pam's face, and she looked back at him with such joy and sadness that he reached for her, terrified that she would fade away in the misty light. Yet he could not touch her. She stayed away from him, shaking her blonde head softly, sorrowfully. But he held on to the tenderness of her blue eyes, for he remembered that most of all.

He cried out to her through his tears as she left him.
But her voice reached his ears even though he could
see her no longer. He listened intently, her words
distinct and frightening. Strangely, she warned him
to leave, that he was in great danger there.

He sat up, dazed; then he rose to his feet, standing
in the darkness of the room. He shook his head, not
knowing if he had been dreaming or not. The others
in the room slept soundly; he could hear their deep
breathing. All was as he'd left it when he went to bed.
He staggered to the window and looked out into the
night.

Outside, the night was clear and starlit. The stars
seemed to be shifting as he watched them, all looking
very strange. They looked like darting points of light
rather than stars. They could be small meteorites, he
decided.

Alec made his way back to bed and lay down, knowing he did not want to sleep if he was going to dream
again.

Suddenly the stillness of the night was broken by
the screeching and jabbering of birds, followed almost
immediately by the barking of village dogs. Alec got
up and went to the window again. Outside, he saw
the dogs whining and running about, acting scared.

Heavy clouds now moved across the sky and Alec
decided that an oncoming storm was causing the animal's strange behavior. He could hear the Black, too,
moving restlessly about his corral. But that was natural
after the freedom he had enjoyed for the last few days.

Alec returned once more to his bed. The dogs were still barking and above all else he could hear the rattle of the Black's hoofs. He would wait a while; then, if the stallion's restlessness continued, he would go to him.

To keep himself awake, Alec thought of the awe in which Alph's clan looked upon the Black. He could understand it. Even though the Indians of America had known horses only since the seventeenth century, they had adopted horses into their ancient myths, tales and legendary lore. Their storytellers, medicine men and artists all gave the horse supernatural powers. Through the Indians' fertile imagination, the horse became a holy steed, born of the gods. No wonder the Black was revered.

Despite the bedlam outside, Alec suddenly felt tired. He was inclined to doze off though he knew he should remain alert. His eyes closed and opened as he fell asleep and awakened in fits and starts.

Later, how long it had been he did not know, he found himself wide awake again. The noises outside, including the sound of the Black's movements, had ceased completely. If anything, it might have been the dead silence that had awakened him. He sat up, his arms huddled about his knees, and listened.

He was consciously aware of some mystery, some physical nearness . . . something on the order of what had happened to him before when he thought he'd seen and heard Pam.

But all was as it should be in the room. He could

make out the dim outlines of the sleeping figures around him. There was nothing at all to be concerned about.

Alec lay back on the floor. He turned over, trying in vain to fall asleep. The very air seemed to be uneasy. He found his head aching when he'd had no headache before. His blood ran hot and cold.

Alec got up and went to the window once more. He watched the silver crescent moon as it appeared and disappeared beneath a churning sea of clouds. In the distance he could see the mountains, some of the peaks cone-shaped and snow-covered, all very serene in the waves of moonlight. The wind came up, a blurred whining sound in his ears.

Suddenly Alec's thoughts were shattered by a sharp tremor that caused him to lose his balance and fall to the floor! Pots and pans rattled in the room, and the walls rippled like the side of a tent in a high wind. Now Alec understood why the Black had been so restless. Animals were known to sense the coming of an earthquake!

The tremor lasted only a few seconds but seemed much longer. Then, as Alec got to his feet, it was followed by a rapid-fire series of five more tremors that threw him down again. He lay there until the tremors ceased. He heard Alph's family running to the door, and he leaped up and followed them into the night.

The Indians were as shaken as Alec. He stood with them in a closely knit group, a terrible sensation of hopelessness and fear coming over him when he saw what had happened to the village.

The shacks were sagging like listing ships and from them men, women and children were still running, crying in alarm. They pulled their possessions behind them.

Alec fought to control his own panic as the earth once more trembled beneath him. He tried to hold his legs steady despite the shaking ground. He was aware that the villagers were gathering nearby, and when he looked at them, he felt a sense of wonder.

They were all standing motionless, their eyes skyward and arms outstretched.

Alec saw what held their gaze. It was the comet he had seen earlier, plunging through the sky like a gigantic rocket and trailing streaks of cold, blue fire.

But now the meteoroid seemed to be traveling toward the earth. The flaming mass grew larger, brighter, before Alec's eyes. He told himself there was nothing to fear from it or anything else in the night sky, ever. Meteoroids burned themselves out when they reached the earth's atmosphere. Earthquakes, too, were to be expected in this area. There had been hundreds of them, reported and unreported. Seldom was there any loss of life.

Alec tried to move away from the others to go to his horse, for above all things he wanted to be with the Black. But he seemed to have lost the power of movement. He felt faint, unsteady on his legs. He wondered what was happening to him. He turned his head to look skyward again.

The star of vivid blue was no longer a great spot of light in the heavens but had grown into an immense splash of flame across the night sky. As he watched, the light grew ever stronger until it was possible for Alec to see every detail in the faces of the people around him.

They actually believed the end of the world had come! Their faces held a wondrous look of preparation and acceptance. Their arms were outstretched toward the flaming meteoroid.

Steadily, the great star increased in size and brilliance, its blue light making the faces of the Indians look unreal. Now the meteoroid was so large that it seemed to fill the whole sky. Its light was a stupendous dome of blue fire.

With sick dread, Alec realized that the meteoroid was going to crash close by, and none of them had a chance of staying alive in the holocaust that must come!

Earthfire!

19

Dropping to the ground, Alec cowered with the others, waiting for the meteoroid to strike the earth. Moments later there came an explosion the like of which he'd never imagined. The very sound of it set off agony and terror within him. His ears ached and rang from the impact. The land lifted and rocked beneath his body and every village shack toppled.

Finding himself still alive, Alec raised his head from where he had buried it against the ground. He was conscious of little but fear. The earth beneath him was tilting upward and outward. He dug his hands into the dirt, as if letting go meant falling into deep space.

Much later he looked up to find the sky clear except for a steady light that swung over the land in mighty arcs. It seemed more a river of flame than any remaining light from the meteoroid.

With awful clearness Alec saw explosive plumes of smoke and ash rising everywhere around, topped by mushroom clouds of steam. Acrid gases filled his nostrils, and in the distance he heard the clatter of a multitude of rockslides.

Alec could only guess that he was in the middle of a great earthquake, perhaps triggered by the meteoroid, with explosions caused by red-hot magma swelling up from the depths. It was his only rational explanation. But what about the river of flame that came and went in mighty swings above him? What had it to do with the upheaval of the earth?

Alec staggered to his feet, determined to reach his horse despite the still-heaving ground. His every step took enormous effort.

Is it truly the end of the world? he asked himself. *Is it?*

The rails of the corral were strewn everywhere, but Alec found the Black standing nearby, his ears turned to each explosion. Alec reached his horse and threw his arms about him. He found the stallion's coat wet with sweat and mud, and his breathing coming heavily.

"You're not alone, not anymore," he told the Black. "Whatever happens, we'll be together."

The earth continued to shake with strong vibrations. The river of flame overhead grew duller and the night became more indistinct. The Black jumped, trying to break away. His horse's fear, Alec knew, was as real as his own. The Black sought escape in frantic flight.

"Not now," Alec told him. "There's no place to run."

Coming toward them were the Indians. Alec couldn't believe they were the same people he had known only moments before. Their shoulders were stooped and their faces wrinkled with the years of a century. Only their eyes were the same—deep, dark coals shining with fervor as they called again and again to him and his horse, "Lead us, Black Fire! Lead us!"

Alec tried to answer, but his own fright made it difficult to breathe let alone speak. He could only look at them, wondering if he appeared as pitiful in their eyes as they did in his. And yet they still had hope of survival, for on their backs they carried all the belongings they had in the world—burlap bags filled with food, ragged clothes, seeds for planting—everything they needed to begin life in their new world.

Finally he was able to speak and his voice was hopeless and bitter. "We can't lead you anywhere," he said.

They had turned from him to look directly overhead. Alec's gaze followed and he saw something luminous and ghostly in the night sky. A bluish flame flickered there, and for a moment Alec thought that the meteoroid had reappeared. He saw a glare of bright fire within the blue flame and then, suddenly, his nose was filled with the stench of burning.

The Black screamed and reared high in the air, trying to break away from Alec. He came down to stand still a moment, his nostrils flared wide from the burning odor.

Alec knew he had to control the Black's panic as well as his own if they were to survive. He knew that death was close to all of them. Somehow he managed to get on the raging stallion's back.

The light overhead became one of dazzling brilliance and the air hot beyond description. This had to be the end of all things, Alec thought, just as the Indians had said.

Screaming in fear, the Black bolted forward, and Alec cried out in defiance of the holocaust.

Then the great curtain of fire overhead grew paler. It slowly turned the land below to a deep copper color with a heavy purple tint that reminded Alec of a dreadful shade of blood, belonging to the last hour of the world.

The sky became dark, making it difficult to see the way ahead. Alec brought the Black to a halt, fighting the stallion, who wanted to run on. Above, the arc of dull flame was only a dim ghost of its former self, and the night became very still and cold.

Alec couldn't believe the air could have changed so rapidly with the darkening sky. Where had the intense heat gone? The night had sunk into frigid black.

Then from somewhere behind him Alec heard muffled voices, followed by loud cries.

"Lead us!"

Alec looked back but could not see the Indians in the dark. He held on to the Black, his thoughts chaotic as he tried to overcome his sense of desolation as well as guilt for leaving them behind.

He could be of no help to the Indians, he told himself. He could do nothing for them. Their fate was no different than his own. It was only a question of time for all of them.

A growing sense of numbness came over Alec. It was a feeling he did not understand but did not challenge. He couldn't account for what he did, but moments later he found himself riding back toward the Indians.

Somehow, what he was doing seemed strangely right to him now. It was as if he were suspended in a dream, viewing everything quite calmly when he should have felt only fear in what he had to do . . . *return to the sacred pueblo.*

The Indians came running toward him, driving their sheep and village dogs before them. Turning the Black, Alec led them through the night and icy cold.

The Beginning of the End?

20

As Alec led the Indians from the mesa, he found that there was no escape from the holocaust. Exposed as they were, with the ground heaving beneath them, he became swathed in terror. He clung to the Black's neck, dazed and exhausted, knowing that when death came it would be at his horse's side.

His eyes turned to the heavens again, and he hoped he had the will to live. The night curtain had opened and he saw stars. Then the starlight dimmed altogether and deep blackness fell once more upon the earth. A vast rain came and Alec clung more tightly to the Black's neck in the drenching downpour. The rain was accompanied by a fierce gale and hundreds of lightning flashes, which seemed to sweep downward in a great shower of flame. Then they were gone and darkness fell once more over the land.

Terrified, Alec waited in the dark. He heard the cries of the Indians behind him but it was useless to try to see them. The blackness, and all that was happening to him, was brutal to his senses. And yet, as he sat on the Black, he took courage in the strength of the great stallion who carried him.

Clouds of vapor rose about them and Alec could hear the tumbling rockslides and avalanches roaring down the mountainsides beyond. He no longer felt any fear of whatever lay ahead. All that was happening to him seemed unavoidable and, somehow, necessary. He closed his eyes in a state of drowsy semi-consciousness. His languor, he knew, must be from the gases rising from the earth, for they made it difficult to breathe. Again he heard the Indians calling to him but he didn't listen to their cries. Solitude and dreariness had replaced his feelings of fear and horror, and for that he was grateful.

The Black moved on as the night lightened from the flares of new explosions. Loud booms shattered the stillness. In the distance Alec saw the towering cliffs of the mountains tremble and then dissolve into a mass of tumbling rocks.

Why would anyone, even the Indians, believe there was a safe haven within that mass of falling stones?

Alec knew there was no rational answer to his question. He held tight to the black mane as more explosions followed. And within the flaring light he saw a fearsome sight.

Coming across the plain, running toward him, was

a legion of painted bodies and faces. The loco brothers! Alec caught his breath sharply as the figures grew steadily before his eyes, a monstrous mob he thought he'd left behind forever! They came ever closer, huge eyes staring wildly at him.

Cold with fresh horror, Alec stared back at them. Then, suddenly, he realized that the eyes staring at him were not hostile but tortured with despair and hopelessness, no different from his own.

Silently, Alec watched them fall in line behind him and the village Indians. Whatever their beliefs had been, they now sought safety in an ancient Indian prophecy.

When Alec neared the mountains, he found that the canyons looked so much alike he could not distinguish one from another. Which one had he used the day before? Or had the numerous rockslides already closed it?

There was a narrow rift directly ahead and Alec rode toward it. As the walls closed over his head, Alec's gaze turned upward at the towering rock. He thought he had chosen the right canyon, leading to the sacred pueblo, but he couldn't believe they would find safety there. The wonder of it was that they had managed to travel this far without being killed.

Beyond, as the canyon widened, Alec saw ground vents spurting geysers hundreds of feet in the air, and the smell of sulfur was strong. The Black came to a sudden stop within the murky veil of vapors, his nostrils quivering. He did not like the smell of fumes any more than Alec did. But he went forward with the pressure of Alec's legs, his hoofs ringing as they struck the stones.

The earth tremors started again, and Alec heard the Indians screaming for him to wait for them. He looked behind and realized that the cries were coming from the painted ones who were far behind in the rear. The main group had stayed close to the stallion's heels, afraid of losing him.

Behind him, Alec saw the walls of the rift tremble with the sharp earth tremors; then, suddenly, the cliffs toppled in, vanishing completely and pouring tons of stone upon those who had lagged behind!

Shocked by what he had witnessed, Alec sent the Black forward at a run. He knew there was no turning back now, *ever*.

Alec recognized the area despite the eruptions. Light played across the sky and he saw that the streambed was not where it had been. Its course had been altered by the quakes. Neither was it dry any longer but half-filled with water from the snows that had cascaded down the mountainsides and melted from the intense heat below.

Alec knew he had no choice but to go forward. He urged the Black on into the shallow water, and the Indians followed. Carefully they picked their way up the streambed, through the long, narrow chasm that Alec had traveled once before.

Finally, in the light of the continuing explosions outside, Alec saw the huge amphitheater of the sacred pueblo ahead. Its grass was as green and lush as when he had left it. To either side the cave dwellings rose tier after tier above the pueblo floor, as secure as they had ever been despite the upheaval of the world outside.

Alec shivered at the knowledge that the sacred pueblo might well be the safe haven the Indians had prophesied. He rode the Black forward as the light faded and the night once more became intensely dark and silent.

Sanctuary

21

For what seemed endless hours, Alec stayed close beside his horse. The Indians had left him to seek security deep in the cave dwellings, and for that he could not blame them.

Many thoughts crowded his mind, but he was able only to stare into the darkness. Would the Indians find their new world? And what about his own world? What *was* happening outside the sacred pueblo? The night had become uncannily still.

Later, how much later he didn't know, Alec found himself walking up the path to the dwelling into which the Indians had gone. It was a tremendous cave, dimly lit from the light of a fire coming from beyond. He went deeper, the dust swirling about his feet and his footsteps echoing softly from the walls.

He found the Indians in a large, circular room, sitting about a great fire, the smoke going up a stone chimney. Splintered, ancient ladders lay broken against the walls, all rising story after story to still more chambers, which loomed above them.

Alec's gaze was attracted to the drawings on the walls of the large room, all showing a lithe, red-skinned people wearing fine, delicate jewelry. In the drawings, too, were sophisticated weapons lying on the ground, and tools and artifacts, all definite examples of an advanced Indian culture.

Was the small group of Indians seated around the blazing fire all that was left of such people?

Alec remained where he was. Who could understand the true meaning of everything these people had endured? What came after the end? A new beginning as they believed?

The smell of their cooking and sounds of life finally penetrated Alec's senses. He walked forward and they raised their poles in greeting. For the first time Alec was aware of the prayer sticks and clan feathers they had brought with them.

The boy, Alph, rose from where he sat beside his parents and moved over to Alec. "Stay with us," he said. "We will greet the new world together." His thin arm went around Alec's waist, pulling him toward the fire. "We will eat and be strong. Then when the new day comes we will begin planting our crops."

For what seemed endless hours, Alec sat beside Alph listening to the Indians' prayers to their many gods—the Sun, the Moon, Earth and Stars—as well as to all the Spirits that could be manipulated through their rituals to provide them with their needs.

The night seemed to be never-ending. Often Alec would awaken from fitful moments of sleep to go to the Black, not only to make certain his horse was all right but to touch him, as though the stallion were the only reality he had left in his world. Then Alec would return to sit with the Indians and listen to their prayers and hopes for the better world to come.

During this time Alec's mind wandered between reality and a dream. Was it somehow the same for him as it was the Indians? Had he wanted to be free from the cruelty of a world that had taken Pam from him? Was that what had brought him here?

Finally Alec staggered to his feet. "Running away, like dying, is easy," he said aloud. "It's the living that's hard." His answer, the only answer to all the pain he had suffered, was to go on. To refuse to leave the safety of the sacred pueblo was to run out on the only world he had.

Alec was on his way out of the cave when he felt Alph's arms around him, attempting to hold him back.

"I'm going," he told the boy. "I've got to find out what's left of my world."

"There is only death outside the pueblo," Alph pleaded, his dark eyes seeking Alec's. "The new day is almost here. You must stay. You are one with us."

"I've never been what you think I am," Alec said. "Neither is my horse . . ."

"That is only what you want to believe. It is not so,"
Alph said solemnly.

"It is all I know to be true," Alec answered, shrug-
ging off the boy's hands. "I can't think of it any other
way."

"Then you will see for yourself," Alph called after
him.

Moments later Alec stumbled from the cave. How
many hours had it been since he'd reached the pueblo?
He'd lost all track of time. His eyes turned to the
narrow opening above and he saw an ever-brightening
patch of gray in the sky. Perhaps Alph was right and
the new day was at hand after all.

Not Alph's new day, he reminded himself, *but the
new day of his own world, not one of an ancient Indian
prophecy.*

A soft wind stirred as Alec made his way down the
path to the floor of the pueblo. The Black grazed nearby,
and just beyond in the ever-growing light Alec made
out the dim figures of the grazing sheep.

Alec moved forward, knowing he had to go on, that
he mustn't stay. Step by step, he made his way to the
Black and threw his arms around the stallion's slender
neck. "As long as I've got you," he said, "we're going
to find our way out of here, Black. We're going
home . . ."

"There Is Only Death Outside"

22

Leaving the sacred pueblo through the narrow chasm, Alec was amazed to find he could look out over the land. The walls of the outer canyons were gone! The morning light was dim but bright enough for him to make out a desolate world. The flattened earth looked dreadful, wrapped in gloom, even death.

Alec stared, passing a hand over his forehead, confused and dazed by what he saw. It all seemed a gigantic dream, a terrible journey through space and time.

How had they survived such a catastrophe even within the confines of the pueblo? Alec gazed in shock at the shattered fragments of rock and debris. Then his wits came slowly back to him, and with it the reality of things.

It was no horrible dream. It had happened, all of

it—the end or the beginning of whatever it might be. For comfort, Alec's arms tightened around the neck of his horse, holding him close.

Alec rode on beneath a sky that was brown-black and a sun that was a dim red glow in the east. Listening, he could hear nothing in the dead silence except his own heavy breathing and the click of the stallion's hoofs on stones.

"Black," he said aloud, "from the beginning I had no right to take you with me."

The stallion's ears turned with the sound of Alec's voice. Then his lofty head turned as well, the large eyes rolling, showing for an instant the crescent white eyeball. A loud snort came from the wet lining of his flared nostrils, as if he understood but would have had it no other way.

A cold wind struck at them and Alec felt the sting of grit against his face. He hunched over, close to his horse's neck, letting the Black find his way through the strewn stone and crumbling debris. He tried to talk to his horse but the grit blew into his mouth when he opened it. So he remained silent, holding the stallion to a walk, trying to see into the wind. As the gusts continued, he tore off what was left of a ragged pant leg and, making a crude mask, covered his face with it.

The minutes lengthened into hours as the stallion scaled the twists and folds of stone, his hoofs kicking up huge clouds of dust. Alec rode with jaws clamped shut to keep his teeth from chattering in the cold. His eyes ached and stung. It was worse for his horse, he knew. Yet they kept going, their bodies stiffening from the cold despite their labors.

Alec looked longingly for the sun, hoping it would bring the true day. It was up there somewhere but it was wasted and sickly behind the brown sky. He could see its edges from time to time, cutting wan patches of broken morning light.

Finally the sky turned amber above the dust-laden air, becoming ruddy and red-edged. It continued to pale, and suddenly darkness left the land as the sun appeared like a round burning hole in the thick dust.

In the first reaching rays of the sun, Alec could find nothing of what he had known before. There was only a dead and ravaged land as far as he could see. The earth was clogged with ash and debris. Trees were uprooted and lying in tangled heaps, their trunks burned and stripped clean. Devastated by violent upheavals of the earth, all the land had an unreal, blasted appearance.

Even the mountains were nothing he had known before. Their summits had collapsed into great steaming depressions with craters gaping miles wide. There was no longer any snow or ice, only gashed remains of the eruptions that had taken place. Domes and peaks had been torn away, and even as he watched, great rock avalanches slid down the sides of remaining cliffs.

The destruction of the land was complete and Alec recalled Alph's warning: *"There is only death outside the pueblo."*

Alec's gaze continued to sweep across the gray and lifeless terrain before him. Could anyone, anything, have survived the awesome force that had caused such destruction?

"But we're alive, Black," he told his horse. "You and I . . . we're going to find someone, somewhere."

Alec rode for a long while before he spotted what looked like the remains of a trail leading down a ridge. Flowing mud and debris poured down to either side of it, but he believed that if he followed it, he might find safety below.

Reaching the trail, he looked for footprints, hoofprints, tracks of any kind. He wished he could find just one person, one animal alive, so he would know he was not alone in his world.

Hearing the rumble of thunder overhead, Alec looked up to see huge, dark clouds sweeping across the sky, driven by what seemed to be hurricane winds. Soon the clouds would blot out the sun and it would be drk again. He moved the Black on while there was still enough light to see his way.

As the great clouds passed overhead, the pale sky turned inky black. There was only a sliver of light on the horizon to the east. Alec rode toward it, guiding his horse carefully, cautiously. A cold wind swept over him and then a fine rain fell.

The rain came down heavier, matting the ash that covered the way before them. The Black's strides faltered, then the stallion stumbled and Alec knew the ground was shifting beneath his hoofs. The horse plunged down the ridge, his way strewn with logs, until he finally reached the bottom.

"Good fellow, good fellow," Alec said. "You made it. It's got to be easier from now on."

Alec rode on, glad for the rain, which cleared the air temporarily of ash and gas. Straining, he pulled clean air into his tortured lungs and knew the Black was doing the same.

Hours later the sun set in the colorless sky and dusk fell upon the ravaged land. Alec didn't know how long he'd ridden when suddenly the Black snorted loudly. Before them Alec saw a sickly lake of gray-brown water where the flow of melted snow had been blocked by mud and the trunks of countless trees.

Reaching the water, Alec slipped off the Black. He felt sick from the vapors that had filled his lungs and parched his throat. He held on to the stallion, both hands around him, his head resting against the hot, sweated side. The rise and fall of his labored breathing matched the horse's. He shook his head, trying to clear it, but his hands trembled and his stomach burned. Gagging, he vomited bloody froth into the dirty mud beside him.

The Black lowered his head to the water, and Alec heard the pulling suck of his lips as the fluid gurgled up the rings of his throat. It sounded good. It sounded wet. Alec decided to take his chances too, for he couldn't feel worse than he did. He dropped to his knees and lowered his head to the water. He tasted its muddy, tepid wetness, letting it run over his tongue and down his throat. He raised his head as his horse did, then dipped to drink again, not swallowing the tepid water this time but rinsing his mouth and squirting water.

Moments later, knowing they could go no farther that night, Alec pulled a canvas bag of parched brown corn from his pocket and, cupping his hand, offered it to his horse.

"Just a little, Black, only a little," he said.

Then, when he took his empty hand away from the soft lips of the Black, he filled it again with corn and wetted it with water. He ate his skimpy meal, knowing there was only enough corn left for another day.

The food stuck sour in his throat as he lay still on the ground, thinking how it had been at home with his horse rubbed down and fed, safe in a stall with clean straw, close beside a tack room with saddles and bridles and the smell of clean, polished leather. Then Alec fell asleep and dreamed as he had not dreamed in years.

He was a small boy and wanted a horse of his own very much, but he lived in a city and could not have one. Then something wonderful happened and he was riding a great, black horse. Someone said in his dream, "You will never be able to ride that horse. You cannot keep him." He cried because he wanted to ride the black horse very much . . .

Alec awoke with a start and there were tears on his cheeks from his dream. He knew it was time to get up and soak his head in the water. There was no need to go back so far, even in dreams.

It was shortly before daybreak, the coldest time of the darkest hour. He got to his numbed feet, shivering and stretching to ease the stiffness from his legs and back. The Black was standing nearby and Alec went to him, holding him close for his love and the warmth of his body.

"It was no dream," he said softly. "You're here, and we're going to find our way out somehow."

Alec mounted his horse and rode from the clearing. By dawn he was climbing the strewn gullies that rimmed the edge of what was left of the trail, his breath smoking in the cold but clean air.

An hour after daylight a strong wind came up and swept across the ravaged land. It blew over the tumbled stones of the mountains and across the bare land, but none of it was as bad as the day before. The trail led downward, ever downward, toward the desert, where Alec knew they would find warmth and, he ped, peace and safety.

The desert loomed before Alec in a fluid tremor of heat, but he welcomed the warmth after the numbing cold he had felt for so long. As the hours passed and the Black traveled through the ever-mounting warmth, Alec knew he wasn't thinking clearly anymore. He had trouble focusing his eyes on the rutted trail ahead. He didn't have to see, he told himself. His horse knew where he was going.

Finally night fell upon them once more and the stars began to show in the sky. A breeze rustled through the brush of a nearby clearing, and Alec smelled water and damp grass.

The Black made his way to a pool of clear water ebbing from the rocks, and there Alec drank with his horse, long and without hurry. They had found their place for another night.

Moments later Alec ate the last of his corn while the Black fed on whatever grass he could find near the water, pulling and munching hungrily, moving faintly in the darkness but never far away.

Alec stretched out on the ground, listening to the muffled sound of his horse's teeth and wondering what they would find beyond.

"Sleep good, Black," he called. Then he fell asleep, hungry.

Sometime during the night Alec felt a prickle-footed thing crawling across his face. He jerked up, slapped it off and jumped to his feet to see a centipede squirming in the earth. He raised his foot to mash it with the heel of his boot. But he could not bring his foot down to stomp it into pulp in the dirt. It was the first sign that life remained in his world.

World Without End

23

An hour after daybreak Alec was on his way again. He had forgotten how long it had been since he'd left the sacred pueblo. Two days? Or was it three?

Suddenly Alec checked the Black's strides; then he bent over to study the trail and, finally, slid from his horse to read the hoofprints deep in the earth.

Shod hoofs! The Black's! They marked the ground in a regular order of strides. Alec studied the soil grains edging the tracks and knew he and his horse had traveled this way when they had first come to this land. He mounted again and rode on eagerly, hopefully.

It was more than an hour later when Alec pulled up the Black again, stopping sharp and squinting into the sun with his hands shading his eyes. He was able to make out the corners of adobe huts and fence posts hidden in the haze beyond. He rode toward the lonely village, thinking of the people he might find there and the food he might get while he was with them . . . meat and tortillas and corn for his horse.

Not a leaf, not a stem, stirred in the sweating hush of the day as Alec neared the settlement. Suddenly the Black stopped of his own accord and stood riveted to the ground. Then he screamed and the sound of his shrill whistle rang through the still air.

Alec saw what lay ahead. There was nothing left of the village. There were no homes, no people. The walls and roofs of adobe shacks were scattered about. Tawny stone, pale mud brick and bodies lay everywhere. He saw the black humps of rubble where the homes had been, the scorched trees, roofless walls, window holes, all in gaping ruins.

The Black was in sudden veering panic, but Alec got him moving forward, sweeping wide of the ruins. As Alec rode away he talked to his horse, more to console himself and to make sense of what he had seen, as much as he was able to do.

"I hope I can tell someone what happened here. I wish I could help everybody who lived here, but I can't. It's over, and I don't know what's ahead."

The wetness of the stallion's neck and the swing and push of his haunches kept Alec conscious, if not alert. He knew he was going to be sick. At every pound of the Black's hoofs he felt his backbone ram into his skull, like a hammer pounding his head. He leaned over and vomited beside the stallion.

"*Keep going or you are done,*" he warned himself.

"You have to find your way to whatever is ahead." He felt the drive of the Black's legs beneath him. He didn't look back.

Two hours passed and Alec held on to his horse with desperate hands and great effort of will. The sun was hot, the going rough. Rocking in the twist of inner as well as outer pain, he tried to throw off the fevered weakness that was slowly overpowering him.

Alec rode across the vast immensity of the desert with its dunes and far horizons. At the top of a sandy rise, he recognized the area as the one in which he had left his truck and trailer so long ago! He squinted in the glare of the sun, trying to find some sign of the vehicles.

Darn his eyes, he couldn't see!

There was a familiar shallow dish in the land to his right. It could be where he'd parked the truck, he decided. It could be, but where was it? He narrowed his eyes still more, trying to see. There, there . . . he thought he saw the outline of something in the sand.

The Black was moving toward the shallow dish of ground, his strides lengthening, his ears pitched forward.

"That's fast enough," Alec cautioned his horse. "Don't use all you got left. You don't need to use it all."

The light from the sun had moved down, reddening the way before them, when Alec reached his truck and trailer buried deep in sand and ash. He rode up to what remained of the hulking body of the engine, then alongside the flattened horse trailer, its body splintered into pieces strewn about the area.

Alec knew he could follow the road that led ever southward, the way they had come so long ago. Eventually he would reach the highway. But had he the strength to go on? Had his horse? And what would they find there? Only death and destruction as well?

Alec's gaze swept over the waste of lifeless desolation all around him. He felt his own smallness under the immensity of it all.

His eyes returned to the shattered body of the horse trailer, then suddenly he slipped off the Black and went to it. Dropping to his knees in the sand and ash, he uncovered one of the pieces that stuck in the earth like a signpost. He read the lettering on it while holding it in the air, high in the sun.

H O P E

It was all that was left of "HOPEFUL FARM" but enough for Alec to know he had to go on, to find his way back to whatever life still held for him.

Alec rose to his feet. The road beyond led down a steep slope to a plateau below. He'd better get going. Before long it would be dark and impossible for him to find his way.

He mounted the Black and rode on, no longer feeling total despair but a glimmer of hope, hope for himself and all mankind. Life without his beloved Pam would always be a kind of doom, he knew. But he had learned that one lives with his loss until it can be accepted, and something that was not his alone but that he shared with Pam would always live within him. He had come to this land seeking peace for his troubled mind. From the Indians, those who had lived and died, he had learned the power of their faith and courage. In many ways, they were showing him the way back home.

Aftermath

24

"This is your emergency radio station in Flagstaff, Arizona.

"Scores of desert and mountain residents are arriving daily, having miraculously survived a mighty earthquake that scientists report to be one of the worst natural disasters in the country's history. The series of huge tremors, which had seismographs quivering at the top of the scale, laid waste to upland areas for hundreds of miles.

"Scientists have calculated that the quake was the longest surface rupture ever recorded from a single fault movement. Further tremors are expected today.

"Scientists have no explanation for the phenomenal blue light that appeared in the sky prior to the tremendous quake and which was seen over a radius of several hundred miles. It has been suggested by many

169

observers that the blue light had something to do with the quake. Scientists have offered no comment on this view.

"Among those arriving safely in Flagstaff was the world-renowned jockey Alec Ramsay and his equally famous horse, the Black. It is not known at this time what they were doing in the desolate desert area.

"Further reports just received state that a series of severe tremors are being experienced elsewhere throughout the United States. The U.S. Geological Survey Office has also reported eight damaging earthquakes around the world . . ."

Alec Ramsay was one of five hundred persons seeking safety in a school gymnasium that was being used as a refugee center by the state Department of Emergency Services. All were homeless and frightened and sat huddled in large groups around cafeteria tables and army cots.

Alec knew the scene was being repeated elsewhere in the city—in gyms, schools and National Guard armories, all filled with refugees forced from their homes and anxiously awaiting word on whether loved ones left behind had lived or died.

Alec had seen the complete devastation of the upland areas with his own eyes and knew how slim the chances of survival were for anyone caught in the holocaust and how quickly death could come. Others would never really know such things. They could only wait and hope.

What can I tell them? he thought. *Only that there's a chance. All they can do is keep praying.*

It was the third day that Alec had been in the shelter and nothing had changed. The sky was dark and ominous and the earth tremors continued hourly as if there were no end to them.

A large tent had been set up just outside the school building for penned and stabled animals. It was there the Black stood in his makeshift stall, listening to the sounds of the other animals. There were eight horses and ponies beside the Black and, Alec counted, fifteen dogs, six cats, three goats, two calves and any number of caged birds.

Alec opened the stall door and the Black came forward quickly, his eyes alert and impatient.

"Not yet, not yet," Alec told him. "There's no place to go."

Alec watched his horse move in the straw, noting how much he favored his left forefoot. He'd suffered several stone bruises but otherwise seemed to be all right. That was the miracle of it all, that they had survived.

Or had they? Alec asked himself. *Was it over?*

More refugees were arriving every hour from stricken areas. Red-jacketed volunteers continued to unload trucks of clothing and food. All were wearing surgical-type dust masks over their faces as protection from the winds, which were still heavy with ash that could clog their lungs.

Top priority, the only priority anyone had, was saving human lives. But in need of solace and comfort, Alec turned to his horse. He bent down in the straw and carefully picked up the stallion's injured foot. It would take time to heal but the injury was nothing, nothing at all. He looked up at the Black's head with its small ears pricked in the direction of the other animals. His only interest was watching them in their pens and cages. There were no signs of restlessness. Even the incessant barking of the dogs didn't seem to bother him. He snorted at them and for a moment their barking stopped, only to begin again, louder than ever.

So the other animals were more of a comfort to the Black than a trial, Alec decided. *The wonder of it all. To go on with life regardless of how bad it had been for them or what dangers lay ahead.* He rubbed the stallion's neck. He had learned a lot from his horse as well as the Indians.

A small group of reporters came toward Alec, their faces grim, eyes darting nervously at the tortured faces of people who wanted more information than they could provide.

"Nothing is left upland," Alec heard one tell a woman. "It's like a huge vacuum that's sucked everything up. There's nothing left, yet there doesn't seem to be an end to it."

Alec didn't want to face the media but there was a chance the reporters had gotten through to the outside world and he desperately needed to know if his parents and Henry were all right.

Serious communications problems had developed from the onset of the quakes. Rescue agencies as well as reporters had tried to use the phones, only to find the lines jammed or down, and there had been little radio communication for the last two days.

"Were you able to get through?" Alec asked. "Do you know what's happening, anything at all?"

"Only snatches on the radio," the reporter answered. "Atmospheric conditions have gone crazy."

"There are reports of quakes being felt from San Diego to Portland," he went on. "They've had two powerful quakes and dozens of aftershocks, just like we're having."

"We're worse off here," another reporter said. "Three hundred square miles of upland homes have been leveled as if they were matchsticks. And that's nothing compared to what the ash and mud are doing to the highways. Everything has ground to a halt. People who aren't already here aren't going to make it at all."

A man in the rear of the group said, "Some people on the radio are talking in terms of biblical wrath or a nuclear Armageddon. They say what's happening is an act of God."

"That's crazy," another said. "It's none of that. It's no different than what we've had in past years, quakes and aftershocks, quakes and aftershocks."

"But never anything like this," the first reporter said vehemently. "It's never been as bad as this. It's not just one area. It's all over, country-wide, even world-wide."

"Yeah," another agreed. "The Associated Press reported that Japan had one of the worst quakes in its history, measuring 8.7 on the scale . . . killed thousands. They don't know how many, and the aftershocks are continuing."

"Russia got it too," someone said. "The World Meteorological Organization reported a major quake that forced the evacuation of all buildings in Moscow and caused fissures in all main highways leading out of the city. There was more but that's all I could get."

"What about our East Coast?" Alec asked. "Have you heard anything?"

"Only snatches like the other reports," the first reporter answered. "They've had one brief quake but it was powerful enough to be felt in a vast stretch from Georgia all the way up to Canada. Police said no deaths have been reported but the aftershocks are continuing about one every hour. So I don't think the East Coast has seen the end of it yet."

Alec thought of his parents and Henry, of Hopeful Farm and the horses. What had happened to them? Would he ever know—or was this truly the end of everything, as the Indians believed?

"Is there no way to get through by phone?" he asked.

"None. What lines aren't down are jammed. Maybe tomorrow . . . or the next day . . . or the one after that." The reporter shrugged his shoulders and moved away. "That's if any of us are around to put in a call . . ."

The newsmen walked away from Alec and the Black. A championship racehorse and his rider held little interest for them at the moment. As it was with all others in the shelter, their only interest was *survival*.

Two days later the aftershocks ceased and with it the sky cleared for the first time. It was late in the afternoon when Alec's turn finally came to use the one phone that had been allotted to the refugees. His hands trembled as he dialed the long-distance number. He listened to the electronic sounds that were taking him ever closer to *home*.

"Keep ringing," he found himself saying. "Keep going all the way. Don't stop now."

At last he heard the final long rings and his heart pounded harder. At least he knew there was still phone service to Hopeful Farm. Some normalcy was returning to his life!

"Hello."

His father had answered. "Dad! It's me, Alec!" There was silence at the other end. "Dad, can you hear me? It's Alec!"

Finally Alec heard his father's voice again, this time weak and far away, as if service was being disrupted.

"Alec, Alec, we thought . . ."

"Don't try to talk, Dad, just listen. I'm okay. I'm in Flagstaff, Arizona. It's been bad, but I think the worst is over. The roads are being cleared and the airport is supposed to open tomorrow . . ."

There was a long pause, then another voice came on the line, garbled yet familiar.

"Alec, this is Henry. Your father is too overcome to talk. He's been sick. He thought you were dead. He's

telling your mother now. Stay where you are and I'll come and get you as soon as I can get out of here. Is the Black with you? Is he alive?"

"Yes, Henry, he's here. He's alive . . . very much alive."

"Speak up. I can't hear you, Alec. There's trouble . . . aftershocks or something, somewhere along the line."

"I said the Black's alive and with me!" Alec shouted.

"I heard you. Good. I'll try to get a cargo plane then. Can you hear me, Alec?"

"Just about. Your voice is getting weaker."

"You stay put, Alec. You hear that? I'll get to you somehow. Don't go running off."

"I won't. I promise. I'm through running. Is it bad there, Henry?"

"Awful. We're starting to clean up. Lots of work but it's not hopeless. Most of the barns are down but fortunately the horses were outside. The house is okay and no one's been hurt. There's a deep fissure where the training track used to be. It's awful but at the same time it's a miracle that we're alive."

Alec could barely make out the old trainer's words when Henry added, *"It looks like we're goin' to have to start all over again, Alec. An' we're lucky to be having a chance to do it."*

Alec hoped the old trainer could hear him, for what he had to say was important to both of them and to the future of Hopeful Farm.

"I want us to go on, Henry!" he shouted at the top

of his voice. "But I want to ride for the joy of riding as I once did, as Pam did, not for the dollars in it."

Henry's voice was very faint but Alec could make out his words.

"Sure, Alec. I understand. I realize now what's important and what isn't. Anyone going through this nightmare would know that. If we survive all this, it might even be good for us, for everybody. We'll all come to our senses as to what it really means to be alive."

"That's the way Pam felt."

"I know, Alec. I know that now."

The floor beneath Alec's feet tilted as a sharp tremor came from deep within the earth.

Alec held on to the phone, knowing this too would pass.

"Henry, can you hear me?"

There was no answer.

AUTHOR'S POSTSCRIPT

This is a work of fiction. While horses appear in the myths and tales of the American Indians, there is no legend to my knowledge that is exactly like the one I have told in this story.

W. F.

ABOUT THE AUTHOR

Walter Farley's love for horses began when he was a small boy living in Syracuse, New York, and continued as he grew up in New York City, where his family moved. Unlike most city children, he was able to fulfill this love through an uncle who was a professional horseman. Young Walter spent much of his time with this uncle, learning about the different kinds of horse training and the people associated with each.

Walter Farley began to write his first book, *The Black Stallion*, while he was a student at Brooklyn's Erasmus Hall High School and Mercerburg Academy in Pennsylvania. He finished it and had it published while he was still an undergraduate at Columbia University.

The appearance of *The Black Stallion* brought such an enthusiastic response from young readers that Mr. Farley went on to write more stories about the Black, and about other horses as well. He now has twenty-eight books to his credit, including his first dog story, *The Great Dane Thor*; the story of America's greatest racehorse, *Man O' War*; and two photographic story-books based on the two Black Stallion movies. His books have been enormously successful in this country, and have also been published in fourteen foreign countries.

When not traveling, Walter Farley and his wife, Rosemary, divide their time between a farm in Pennsylvania and a beach house in Florida.